M000304431

Daughter of the Damned

Daughter of the Damned

J. Boyett

SALTIMBANQUE BOOKS

NEW YORK

Typeset by Christopher Boynton

Saltimbanque Books, New York
www.saltimbanquebooks.com
jboyett.net

ISBN: 978-1-941914-10-6

For Leo and Mary.

For Chris Boyett, Pam Carter, Dawn Drinkwater, and Andy Shanks.

Acknowledgments

Many thanks to Kelly Kay Griffith for her help with the manuscript.

Daughter of the Damned

One

The young woman awoke with a start, her dreams boiling over the lip of her mind till they broke through her sleep. The glass amplified the sun's heat as it came pouring through the window, but that wasn't the only reason she sweated. As usual, a wash of relief came as she realized she'd been dreaming. She remembered where she was and why, and took note of the fact that the car wasn't moving and that her companion was gone. Getting out and stepping onto the otherwise deserted highway, she found the older woman changing the tire. She must have slept through the car being jacked up. It seemed funny that someone would raise a car up on a jack without asking its occupant to get out first.

"You need help?" asked Carol, shielding her eyes from the sun with her hand as she looked down at the other woman. The calm auditory violence of the cicadas droned on and on from the surrounding woods.

Her companion, Snake, grinned up at her. She made a contrast to the young, blonde Carol. Snake wore sturdy jeans, a flannel shirt, and despite the heat a multipocketed olive vest. Also a multipocketed utility belt. She was by no means fat, but a lot bulkier than Carol. Her short copper hair was graying, and she didn't bother holding a hand up to protect her eyes from the sun. "You're paying," she said, as she fitted on the spare tire.

"Not for this."

"I'm kind of a full-service deal."

On the road again, Carol gazed pensively at the woods blurring past. Snake kept looking away from the empty blue highway to glance at her. Carol wasn't paying attention, so she didn't see the amused glint in Snake's eye, but if she had she

3

wouldn't have paid it any mind. She had never seen Snake when she didn't look amused.

"Not to get personal," Snake said at last. "But what did this guy do, anyway?"

Carol's flesh felt like it was retracting inward, as if she were literally getting smaller. "I thought it didn't matter why."

"Oh, it doesn't. I'm just yapping. Making conversation, killing time. Also I'm curious. I did some looking into this guy, as prep work. And found some interesting stuff. Actually I found very very little overall. That by itself is pretty interesting. And then what little bit I did find was even *more* interesting."

The bounty hunter paused, glanced over at Carol again. When the young woman didn't volunteer anything, it only made her grin wider. Trying a different tack, she said, "So anything in particular you want me to do? Any special requests?"

At first it seemed like Carol really hadn't noticed Snake's question. But then she said, with the defiant determination of a girl who's self-conscious of how funny she sounds saying such things, "I'm going to tear his toes out by the roots."

Snake barked an approving laugh. She reared back and did a double-take, making a show of being impressed. "Whoa!" she said. "Ever do anything like that before?"

Carol recoiled. Her mouth twisted with the same shocked horror as if Snake had flashed her.

Snake asked, "Want to do that yourself, or want me to handle it for you?"

Carol scowled back out her window. "I'll do it," she muttered.

Less than an hour later they pulled over onto the shoulder, not having seen any signs of habitation. Abandoning the rented car, Snake led Carol through the trees. The bounty hunter wore a long canvas bag slung over her shoulder and across her back. Also two handguns holstered at her back, with the utility belt slung underneath. Carol had a Bowie knife in a sheath at her belt. She felt ridiculous carrying it, but Snake had insisted. The woods had that eerie vibrant emptiness of places that are filled with living things but devoid of fellow humans. They came to a fence topped with coils of razor wire and bearing signs every few feet warning TRESPASSERS WILL BE SHOT! Snake pulled a pair of bolt cutters out of one of her vest's compartments and made a hole through the fence for them to pass through.

They continued on their way, leaves crunching underfoot. Carol couldn't figure out how Snake was able to move so much more quietly than her. She thought about all the signs threatening to shoot trespassers, but if Snake wasn't going to show concern, then neither would she. She didn't want Snake to think less of her, to think she was a coward.

Snake held up her hand. "Wait here," she said, without turning to look at her client.

"Why? What is it?"

"Some of our friend's interestingness. Wait here. Don't move—not a muscle."

Snake crept forward. She reached down for a very long stick, a skinny fallen branch, and instead of straightening up again she kept lowering herself onto her belly. She crawled forward like her namesake. After a while, she reached out with the branch.

Carol peered at the end of the branch, squinting to see more clearly. She was surprised by a glint, near the tip of Snake's probing stick, and awed that Snake had been able to pick out that one detail from the profusion of the whole forest.

Snake used the end of the branch to tickle the glinting thing, at just about the same moment that Carol realized it was a wire. No sooner had Snake tickled it, than a blur of activity whooshed out of a nearby tangle of foliage.

Despite Snake's instructions, Carol couldn't help but jump back a few paces. Only after it was all over did her brain manage to put together what had happened: a curved, sharpened stick had burst out of the pile of brush camouflaging it. The cruel spike was attached to some sort of rotating joint, whose force had been released when Snake had touched the wire.

"What the fuck is that?!" gasped Carol.

Snake got back to her feet and brushed herself off, looking at the deadly thing like she approved of its craftsmanship. She winked at Carol. "Didn't you ever see *Conan the Barbarian*?"

"It's a booby trap," said Carol.

"Well, yes. Our friend doesn't want anyone poking around. Now, step where I step. *Exactly* where I step."

And for emphasis, Snake pointed; Carol followed the line of her finger, and saw another tripwire glinting in the sunlight. Snake started off again, giving the second wire a respectful berth.

Carol followed. "But ... shouldn't we disarm this trap, too? In case somebody else comes along?"

Snake cocked an eyebrow at Carol over her shoulder. "Well. *We* don't want anyone poking around, either."

To Carol, the going felt more arduous, now that she was on the look-out for wires. It didn't seem to bother Snake. A quarter of an hour later Snake gestured at Carol to slow down. Snake crouched low and continued on her hands and knees up the gentle slope to a low tangle of bushes, weeds, dead wood and vines. Carol got on all fours and crept up to peer alongside her through the brush.

Atop the mild rise was a clearing, almost a grassy plateau. In the middle of that clearing, a house. A cabin, of unpainted wood. Carol supposed it was pretty roomy for a one-person cabin. It didn't look unpleasant. There was even a porch, with an old-fashioned rocking chair on it.

"Okay," whispered Snake. "There's no electronic surveillance around here—"

"How do you know that?" interrupted Carol, also whispering.

Snake tapped one of her many bulging pockets. "I got a little doodad in here that I checked with."

"When? I've been watching you the whole time, and I never saw you check anything."

"And that's why I get paid the big bucks, hon. Now, as I was saying. There's no surveillance, so he doesn't know we're coming. You wait here and don't make a peep. I'll run up there—once I've got him contained I'll signal you to follow. As long as he doesn't peek out his window at the wrong moment, I'll have the element of surprise...."

The door of the cabin flew open and a man appeared brandishing a shotgun in their direction. Carol felt all her innards being squeezed in a fist: *That's him! That's what he looks like!* The impression he made in her mind was out of all proportion to his quite ordinary appearance: a boyish face, average height, moderately fit, hair just beginning to thin. A baby face, really—he looked much younger than Carol knew him to be. He wore a white T-shirt and pale blue boxer shorts.

He called out in a scared and shrill voice: "Who's there?! Somebody out there?!"

Carol could hardly breathe. Despite what Snake had just said, their quarry was pointing the shotgun right at them.... So much for no surveillance.

It was almost as if he'd had some sort of second sight.

"All right," he called, his thin nasal voice grinding down to a grimmer pitch. "I guess it's a good thing there's nobody in those bushes, since that way it won't matter when I start shooting into them...."

"Wait!" Snake shot upright, her hands in the air. Carol gaped up at her, before nervously following suit. Snake's voice had been a helpless squeal, entirely alien to the soldier of fortune Carol had come to know.

"C'mon, please don't shoot us!" pleaded Snake. The man's nervous eyes jittered back and forth between the two women. "Why would you shoot us?! We just, our car broke down, we're looking for help!"

"How'd you even get here?!" demanded the man.

"There was a hole in your fence."

His mouth pulled down in unbelieving disdain. "*Where* is there a hole in my fence?"

"I don't know, man, back there where we came in!"

"Well didn't you see all those signs warning trespassers would be shot?"

"Yeah, but why would you shoot *us*?! I mean, we're *ladies*! We're just *ladies*!"

The terror in Snake's voice, so unexpected, was almost enough to panic Carol too. Like a child seeing her mother crumble.

It also affected the man up on the porch; but in his case it made him relax his vigilance. Just a bit—his mouth stayed hard, but his eyes softened, and the shotgun drifted an inch or so to the side, till it no longer pointed straight at the women.

Carol barely noticed the shift in the shotgun's position. Snake definitely did, though. Too fast for Carol to follow, Snake whipped a handgun out from the back of her waistband and shot towards the house. Carol jumped, and by the time she clapped her hands over her ears, Snake was already most of the way up the slope. The man, Harold, stood there stunned, with empty hands and wild eyes. Carol was just figuring out that Snake had shot the gun out of his grasp when the bounty hunter reached him, with a punch to the gut that doubled him over and set him retching. "Tricked you, asshole," she said. "Get the fuck in there. *Get* in!"

And Snake had Harold inside the cabin before Carol could even manage to get around the thick underbrush they'd been hiding behind. No doubt about it, she told herself as she hurried up to the cabin, Snake was a mighty effective bounty hunter. Carol was pretty sure she'd even spotted some rope going around Harold's wrists as Snake herded him into the house.

Two

By the time Carol got inside the cabin Snake already had the guy trussed up and gagged, and Carol had nothing to do but look around while Snake tied him to a wooden chair. There were some standing lamps, but for now the only light came through the windows. On the floor were piles of books, mostly battered paperbacks. A tan La-Z-Boy, a battered dark-blue sofa. Propped up in the corner was an AR-15—it turned out that was what had been in Snake's canvas bag. An old TV in one corner, resting atop a combination DVD player/VCR. Flanking the TV were stacks of DVDs and VHS videocassettes. Carol couldn't remember the last time she'd watched something on videotape, and she wondered how long Harold had been holed up here.

As she'd approached the cabin, she'd gotten a better look at the lay of the land. The clearing was a grassy patch of a little more than two acres; the cabin was near the trees, at the edge of the clearing. It had been built on a slope. The slope leveled off and the clearing was a very low plateau; it reminded Carol vaguely of old Native American burial grounds, except it was only a piddling height. There were a couple of sheds in the clearing.

Dusk was sliding into dark, so Carol turned on one of the lamps. Then, thinking of what they were about to do, she drew the curtain.

Snake was bending over, leaning her hands on her knees and smiling into Harold's frightened face. She turned to smile up at Carol. Once again, Carol envied her cool, even if the older woman did frighten her. She didn't even seem winded after having subdued Harold. "Anything you want to say to him?" asked Snake, pleasantly.

Carol could only stand there and glare at him, and breathe. It wasn't that she was breathing faster; but she felt like the air had gotten thicker, so she had to spend more effort to drag it in and push it out.

"Anything you want to *do* to him?" asked Snake. "I could take his shoes off."

Harold couldn't speak because of the ball-gag. He looked a bit more worried and confused than before, at this mention of the shoes.

Snake looked a moment longer at Carol. When she still didn't say anything, Snake turned back to Harold. "Man, I am so curious about you," she said. "Because my client here, she seems like a very sweet girl. A much more stand-up sort of person than I usually get hired by, you know? So I keep asking myself, just what the fuck could you have done that got her so riled up?"

They got the impression that a long list of possibilities was scrolling past Harold's panicked eyes. As if there was a whole shitload of people out there who might want vengeance for something.

Snake turned to look Carol up and down, scrutinizing her. "He doesn't know who you are," she observed. "Y'all have never met."

Carol shook her head. She didn't say a word. She couldn't have if she'd wanted to. The pressure inside her was building so much, her jaws were grinding together so tight, that it felt like her teeth might shatter.

"Well, introduce yourself," said Snake, getting bored. "It's no fun killing a guy, if he doesn't know why you're doing it."

Carol walked to a spot just in front of him. She stepped carefully, afraid that otherwise she would lose control. Harold's wary eyes followed her. Drawing herself up, she said, "My name is Carol Sullivan. You, Harold Moncrief, raped my mother Theresa Sullivan, before I was born."

At the mention of the name "Sullivan," Harold's breathing stopped; and then when Carol spoke her mother's full name, he pressed himself back against the chair, away from her.

Snake draped a friendly arm around his shoulders and placed her mouth close to his ear. "Shit, Harold. You know her face and her name now. I'm worried that's not gonna go well for you."

Carol swallowed, then forced herself to keep going, to finish the statement she'd planned for so long. "I guess Mom shouldn't have told me about all that stuff. I guess it probably fucked me up, me hearing about all that from the time I was a little kid. But I don't want to judge her. Because you're supposed to be generous with the dead. When I was still pretty young she finally got around to slitting her wrists. Don't ask me why I waited so long to hire someone like Snake to track you down."

Snake said, "Now you know *my* face and name. This really is not gonna end well for you, Harold. Nice of you to set yourself up way the hell out here, where no one will ever hear you screaming."

Harold started shaking and lurching back and forth, trying to break free. There was no way he would get loose from Snake's knots, unless he managed to bust apart the chair.

Snake looked Carol up and down, took in the way she stood there fuming, fists clenching and opening, the way the energy crackled around inside her, unable to find an outlet. "C'mere," she encouraged. "Don't you want to give your mom's old friend a love pat?"

Carol was quivering, but otherwise could not move.

"All this way!" cried Snake, in derision and disbelief, and always with that note of mocking amusement underneath. "After coming all this way! After all your big talk! And after the shit he did to your mom!"

Carol pushed herself forward and slapped Harold across the face. The blow connected awkwardly and glided off, like a blow from someone who hadn't ever hit anyone before. But the slap affected Harold out of all proportion to its force. He howled through his gag, and tossed himself about more desperately than before. Snake had to grab the chair to keep it from toppling. "You're kind of a pussy, aren't you?" she said.

11

Carol had hopped back, alarmed by Harold's reaction. Snake cried, "Hit him again! Jesus, have some balls! The fuck's the matter with you?"

Biting her lip, Carol advanced on Harold again and once again hit him in the face. This one connected better. That undammed a flurry of blows, and Carol's hands flew like a small flock of maddened birds, right and left both beating Harold on the face and the shoulders, with open palms or the backs of her hands because it hadn't occurred to her to try making fists. The only sounds were the soft cracks of her hands on him, the creakings of the chair, his muffled mournful groans, and her wet gasps. At the end Carol stepped back again, struggling to catch her breath, staring at Harold with hurt red eyes, exhausted emotionally if not yet physically.

Snake watched her. "You done?" she asked. When Carol didn't reply, Snake shrugged and began undoing Harold's gag, saying, "Well, maybe listening to our friend here go into details about how he did your mom'll inspire you. C'mon, buddy, tell us all about it. Feel free to throw in some begging, but I warn you—you don't get to the good stuff soon, I'm gonna make you regret it."

Gag out of his mouth, Harold coughed, then croaked out, "Don't let her touch me! Don't let her touch me!"

"Kinda would go against my whole reason for being here," Snake said apologetically.

"Don't let her touch me! Please! I'm serious!"

Furious, Carol slugged him in the cheek, hard enough to hurt her hand. "You beg *me*, asshole!" she shouted. "*Me*, not her! *I'm* paying! She was *my* mom!"

The baby-faced man was crying, eyes and face wet, mouth gasping in despair. "No, *please*, really! I understand. I understand. Let her kill me, that's fine, I deserve it. But don't *you* touch me, or we'll both regret it!"

A pause. Snake gave Carol a quizzical look, and she returned it blankly. They still planned on hitting the guy, but what he'd just said was so weird that they had to stop and think about it.

12

Snake turned back to Harold. "So, you can't stand being touched by my friend Carol here, even though you otherwise don't mind dying. Is that, like, because of guilt, or something?" Her tone made it sound like guilt was an exotic concept she'd heard of, and this type of behavior seemed to fit accounts of it.

Harold heaved a sigh, almost a sob, and rocked his head back and forth. "You won't understand," he moaned. "But you really should trust me." Then he added bitterly, "Although it's probably too late now, anyway."

"Too late for what?" demanded Snake, bewildered.

Outside, in the distance, something roared.

All three humans froze. Harold was the first to move again: a jerky spasming as he tried to break free.

Snake reached around to put her hand on one of the guns holstered at the small of her back. "The fuck you got out there?" she demanded. "A guard lion? On steroids?"

Carol gazed at the window as if she could see through the curtain to the source of the noise. She had most certainly never heard anything remotely like it, yet it somehow gave her a familiar feeling....

Harold pitched himself back and forth, making a high keening noise that morphed into a frantic breathless mantra: "...letmegoletmegoletmegoletmego...."

"That another one of your booby traps, Harold?" asked Snake, curiously.

"Let me go!" he sobbed.

Snake put the barrel of her gun against his temple. "Whatever it is you've got out there, tell me how to neutralize it." Her voice was relaxed and conversational. "Otherwise I'm gonna bust your jam-jar."

"I don't give a fuck if you kill me." He turned and looked at the barrel, and suddenly didn't seem quite so confident in that sentiment. But he did say, "I can't see that thing again. Please. I came all the way out here to get away from it! To hide from it so it could never find me again."

"Hide from *what*?" insisted Snake.

13

The very idea of trying to describe the thing set him off all over again. "You'll never believe me!" he shrieked.

Snake hit him in the head with the flat of her hand. Unlike Carol's barrage, Snake's blow was precise and cold. Harold's head reeled—he was stunned, but only for a moment. Snake had too finely calibrated a touch for her to put a guy out of commission, if she didn't want to.

"Try me," she said mildly. Another roar, much closer, though still far away. Snake had said a lion on steroids, but it sounded more like a dozen lions smushed together, each one with a fistful of nails up its ass.

Carol didn't even glance at the window this time. Instead, she stared at Harold. He caught her look and calmed a bit. With a nod, he said, "*You* know."

"I don't know anything."

"But you know there's something *to* know. You can feel the connection. Tell your friend to cut me loose and I can get us out of here." Carol took a step in his direction; his newfound cool evaporated as he drew back and yelped. "Don't *touch* me! Not *you*! You make it stronger, and you help it find us!"

"What does that *mean*?!"

Outside there was a tramping, there was the scream of splitting wood as trees were broken apart and knocked over; the floor vibrated as if there were a dinosaur approaching. Keeping her gun out, Snake took Carol's arm. "Command decision," she said. "We get the fuck out. You're my client, so I'm saving your life. Harold, I was contracted for a customized personal job, but it looks like I'm gonna have to outsource you to your pet bear out there or else give you a quick one in the back of the head." To Carol, as if she were offering a choice of desserts, she said, "What'll it be, hon?"

As Snake drew Carol back they passed behind Harold. He twisted around in his chair, straining to turn his neck back far enough to catch Carol's eye. "You've been having weird dreams, right?" he called.

Carol broke free from Snake's grip and marched back to him. "What did you say?"

"You've been having weird dreams," he repeated. "Let me die and you never find out what they mean."

The rhythmic crashings boomed closer, got louder, the cabin shook more. A bluish glow began to swell through the curtain. Snake hefted her AR-15. "It's on us!" she shouted.

She was about to say something else, but they never found out what that was going to be because the wall disintegrated.

If it had exploded so that the debris blew inward, the shrapnel probably would have killed them. But instead the whole wall was swept to the side, out into the woods. As if something big had taken its paw and swept it out of the way.

The wall gone, they saw the something big. Only it was hard to *see* it, exactly. It was hard for the mind to take its boiling details and collate them into something coherent.

Whatever it was, once it saw them it reared back and screamed an atomic howl of triumph, rage, and hate. All of them, even Snake, were mesmerized a moment by the sight of it.

It was a seething phosphorescent blue-tinted mass; its ectoplasmic body was translucent, but the pulverized wall proved it could be solid enough when needed. Right now its bulk was higher than the eight-foot ceiling; their view of most of it was obstructed, but they got the impression of a hump-like body, like a miniature brontosaurus. Right now it had three thick legs that they could see, but other limbs seemed to be trying to seethe into existence from its electric blue depths.

But that face was what got Carol. It bubbled and changed and shifted position—but basically it was a human face. When the thing knocked the wall out of the way, it was the face that came into the house to look for them, extending out from the long tube of a prehensile neck. And when the creature reared back to give that scream of triumph, it did so by drawing the neck all the way back into its body so that the vicious head was affixed to its bulk, like a three-D psychedelic Shroud of Turin.

It was a face that Carol thought she recognized.

Snake recovered from the shock. She stepped in front of Carol and began spraying bullets into the monster. Apparently it was solid enough to feel them, for it shrank back a couple of yards into the night and screamed in pain. "Go!" shouted Snake.

Carol snapped out of her trance and prepared to follow Snake's order. As she turned to run, her eyes happened upon Harold's. He pleaded with her silently. Without thinking, Carol took out her knife and sawed through his bonds.

The monster only allowed itself to be driven back to a certain point, and when it began to advance again despite the gunfire Snake decided to get the fuck out of Dodge. She noticed that Carol had freed Harold and that he was staggering out of his chair, but she only shrugged disapprovingly. Grabbing Carol by the arm, she said, "Come *on*," and began dragging her to the other side of the house. Carol let the knife clatter to the floor, too freaked out to put it back in its sheath.

Even before they'd turned away from the monster, they knew they were too late. It was squeezing its way in, the ceiling buckling and breaking apart. If the thing didn't catch them it would still knock the cabin down before they could get out of it. But Snake tugged Carol by the arm again anyway, to get her to concentrate on surviving at least until they were dead.

Then, behind them, they heard a voice cry, "Hold!" It took an instant to recognize it as Harold's (though there wasn't anyone else it could have been); it was uttered in a tone different from any they'd yet heard from him; it sounded like it had been electronically treated somehow. They looked back.

And paused, once again stunned. Harold was standing up out of a crouch, drawing back the hand he'd extended. The monster leaped at him in rage, and Carol and even Snake flinched. But the monster bounced off something, even though there was nothing there for it to bounce off of.

Except there was: a shimmering haze, a curtain of light just a touch bluer than the light around it, with just a hint of glitter. The monster threw its growing bulk against the barrier, and roared in frustration as it bounced off again. The women heard the impact: a weird noise, like the sound of a rock hitting a sheet of plexiglass, but fed into a synthesizer and subjected to distortion and echo effects.

The monster kept growing, its bulk tearing up the cabin, and the cracks in the ceiling above it were spreading till they were on the humans' side of the force field, as well. Snake gave another tug on Carol's arm, and grabbed Harold, too—after seeing his force field, she seemed to have decided he might be worth saving, after all.

They burst out the back door into the twilight as half the house came crashing down behind them and the monster roared again. Only after they were outside did Carol realize Snake had known exactly where the back door was. Somehow, without Carol ever noticing, Snake had checked the place out and made a mental map of it.

Snake pointed to the woods and said, "Come on! We can hide there...."

But Harold cried, "No!," and the women both paused. Almost against their will, they had realized that Harold knew more about this threat than they did, and that if they wanted to stay alive they ought to listen to him.

He pointed to a trapdoor maybe fifty yards away from the cabin, down the slope of the clearing and at the very edge of the trees. It was barely visible. "We can hide in there!"

"That fucker'll get through that little door just by breathing on it!" objected Snake.

But Harold was already racing for the trapdoor, and Carol was right behind him—maybe because she believed that he could keep her alive, maybe because she didn't want to let him escape. Snake hesitated, then followed.

Carol put on a burst of speed to catch up with Harold. He twisted around and yelped "Don't touch me!" so forcefully that she jerked back. Only after he'd regained his lead did she remember that she'd come here not only to touch him but to *kill* him, and she angrily sped up again.

The trapdoor led into a kind of cellar—she clambered down its ladder seconds after he had. Her first reflex was to

17

grab him—but he held up his hands, and his face had such a pleading look that she relented, hanging back, breathing hard in confusion.... A pleading look, and perhaps also a warning one.

Snake came sliding down the ladder, slamming the door shut above her. "That door will never stand up to that thing," she said again to Harold. "So I hope you had a good reason to stop by."

"Don't worry," gasped Harold. "This place is a Refuge."

"Like I said, I hope you're right."

"No, no—a Refuge, with a capital R. That's a technical term."

Carol looked at Snake, puzzled. "How come you followed us?" she asked. "You could have saved yourself, in the woods."

"Hey, that thing out there is enough to pique anyone's curiosity, and your little friend here seems to know something about it. And besides, you're my client.... How come *you* followed him instead of me, if you think I'm the one who's better at staying alive?"

Flustered, Carol let her eyes drop. She didn't want to admit to Snake that she would follow Harold into places a lot worse than this, if he really could explain her recent dreams. *And I'm still going to kill him, too,* she promised herself.

She turned to Harold. "A 'technical term,'" she repeated. She spoke as brusquely as she could, so that the evil pathetic fucking rapist would know she hadn't forgotten why she was here. "What does that mean?"

"Technical, as in it has a particular meaning among mages." He saw Snake's blank look, and tilted his head curiously at Carol. "Magery? You know? I mean, you *do* know what your mom was into, right?"

"Don't talk about my mother, shithead."

"Well, all right, but that'll make it harder for me to explain about that thing out there."

It chose that moment to roar again. They felt the ground and the walls vibrating as it passed nearby. Carol raised her forearms over her head, afraid the ceiling would fall in, and Snake fingered the trigger of her rifle.

"Don't worry," Harold assured them. "The creature can't tell we're here, and can't even really see the trapdoor at all. That's what it means, that this is a Refuge. The only catch is if you touch me." He said this only to Carol; Snake was not included. "That'll cut through the spell like a lighthouse lamp through a fog."

"Pretty convenient for you," Carol scoffed.

"Spell, huh," said Snake.

Carol turned to the bounty hunter, embarrassed. "My mother was a … well, she was a witch. I know that sounds crazy and I don't expect you to believe me, but she was."

Snake shrugged equably. "Hey, I've been hired for a lotta weird jobs and seen a lotta wild shit, and the only thing I'm skeptical about is promises. A couple years ago I got hired to put down a vampire—or, well, not technically a vampire I guess, but it *was* a demon that fed off blood. Besides, did you get a load of that thing out there? I think it might just possibly be supernatural." Before Carol could decide whether she was bullshitting about the vampire, Snake slid her gaze toward Harold. "And you know how to handle that big momma. Pretty nifty trick, with the force field. Makes me wonder why you didn't use it on me."

Harold opened his mouth, then snapped it shut. Carol had the impression that he'd been about to explain why his powers were useless against Snake, but had thought better of it. Seeing Snake's tight, knowing smile, she guessed the older woman had interpreted it the same way.

What mattered was that they *were* useless, Carol supposed.

Snake said, "So you seem scared of this thing, but not particularly surprised by it. You been in this fix before?"

A shudder went through Harold, and he bit his lips to stop their trembling. He cleared his throat, and rasped, "Yeah. Fifteen years ago." He looked at Carol. "That was when your mom killed yourself. Am I right?"

Carol ground her jaws and blinked back tears. They weren't tears of grief for her mother; they were tears of powerlessness. "I didn't come to answer *your* questions," she said. "And

19

especially not about my mom. I came here to get back at you, for what you did."

Perversely, Harold really did look like he sympathized with her. If she hadn't known anything about him, she would have taken him for a decent guy who was sorry to see her in a tough spot. The only way that could make sense would be if everything she thought about him were wrong, if her mom had for some sick reason fed her a vile lie that had resulted in Carol giving up everything to come out here and exact an unwarranted vengeance; that would be one final, ultimate humiliation at the hands of her mom. That was the only thing that made sense … and yet it couldn't be that, because she'd confronted the guy with her accusation and he hadn't pleaded innocence. There was a fundamental disconnect between the kind of person he seemed to be, and the heinous crimes he was tacitly admitting to.

In any case, if she wanted answers they would have to come from him. And all of a sudden it felt like she was his prisoner, instead of the other way around.

Three

Snake wandered through the cellar, casually taking inventory. The place had a dirt floor. Naked bulbs hung from the low ceiling and provided the only illumination. It was crammed full of wooden shelves, weathered but sturdy. Stacked on the shelves were all sorts of knick-knacks: dried herbs, glass jars containing colored liquids or animal parts floating in formaldehyde, tanned furs, wooden fetishes, things made of exotic feathers sewn together, and so on. Hundreds of things. Neither woman could see any rhyme or reason to their arrangements. Snake regarded all the junk with friendly interest, but was too sensible to start messing with stuff she didn't understand.

As she snooped, she talked to Harold. "So you made it sound like that thing outside has something to do with Carol." She still carried the AR-15. She didn't point it at Harold, but it would have been hard for him not to notice how her finger stayed near the trigger. "Explain that."

Harold drew a breath to reply; it was a shuddery breath, and instead of speaking he let it out with a weak sigh. Snake frowned at him. Both women noticed that he glistened with sweat, and that he was trembling. "What's up with you?" demanded Snake.

"Sorry," he said. "Just, throwing up that force-field took a lot out of me. I'm not the mage I used to be."

"Tell me about that thing's face," said Carol, trying to keep all emotion from her voice.

He gave her a hard-to-read look. "Well," he said. "You saw its face, yourself."

For once, the other two were in on something Snake hadn't noticed, and she took a step toward them, curious. "I noticed it

21

had what looked like a human face," she said. "Just figured that was one more bizarre detail among many."

Harold waited. When Carol didn't volunteer anything, he said, speaking to Snake but keeping his eyes on Carol, "If you got a good look at that face, maybe you noticed a family resemblance with your friend here."

Startled, the bounty hunter stared at Carol. "Shit," she muttered, like she was kicking herself for having missed it. "You're right."

"Why did it look like her?" Carol tried to make her voice sound dangerous.

"It's a pretty complicated story," said Harold.

From outside came another deafening roar and the sound of the monster tramping. But it was moving away from them, and soon they heard the trees on the far side of the ruined cabin crashing down.

"Well, stoke the campfire," said Snake. "Because if this place can really hide us from that thing, then we are gonna be here a while."

Harold dropped his eyes, cleared his throat a couple times, and turned red. The color change was noticeable, because he'd been so pale after his confrontation with the monster. The man was blushing.

A murderous impulse pushed its way up from Carol's belly. This little fucker in his T-shirt and boxers didn't get to do something as dainty as blush over the fact that he'd raped her mom.

At last he said, "I guess I'll just start with the basics of what the thing is. Your mom wanted revenge on me because … well, you know why. About fifteen years ago I got a letter in the mail, with a fake return address. Turned out to be enchanted. When I opened it there was dried blood on the inside of the envelope and on the sheet of paper it contained. Nowadays I would check for that kind of thing before touching any piece of mail, but back then I didn't think. There was nothing written on that sheet of paper. There didn't need to be.

"The way the spell worked was, once our flesh came into contact—my flesh and Theresa's, in the form of that dried blood—it conjured the beast. The conjuration, that is. Which then tried to destroy me. Now, an enchantment like that requires the sacrifice of a soul, and you get the most potency out of the soul of the spellcaster. Since the thing was pretty damn potent, and your mom was the likeliest spellcaster, I figured out that she must have killed herself. As part of the conjuring ritual. I barely faced it down and got out alive—if I hadn't had the help of a coven I used to hang out with, I wouldn't be here now. Me and one of the witches in it were … well, we were friends."

Carol felt dizzy. "If my mom gave her soul to that thing out there, does that mean that thing *is* my mom?"

Harold squirmed. "That's a very complicated, technical, philosophical question that I'm not sure I'm smart enough for. But the short answer is 'no.'"

"How come Carol touching you triggered it?" asked Snake.

"It's conjured by contact between my flesh and Theresa's flesh. But according to the creature's mystical logic, there's no substantive difference between the mother's flesh and the daughter's."

"Hey, asshole, quit using my mother's name," said Carol. "You don't get to do that. And explain to me why we're hiding, and why we don't toss your ass out? The whole point of coming out here was to get vengeance for my mom. Now that I find out she's already trying to do it on her own, why am I getting in her way? Why don't I just put my hands on you and ring the dinner bell?"

She stood up, like she was about to do just that. She wasn't sure whether or not she would actually follow through—true, it was what she had come for, but there was something daunting in the idea of actually stepping forward and in cold blood taking action to end a person's life. Here she was at the moment of truth, and she felt her face burn as she realized she might not be tough enough for it.

Harold shrank away from her. "You don't want to do that," he warned, his voice going up in pitch. "The goal of that creature is not just to kill me—its drive is to destroy the trauma of, uh, of what I did to your mother. To symbolically destroy it. And the victim of a trauma is a *part* of that trauma. I mean, no matter what, I end up dead, so I'm not sure whether that's a subtlety your mom just didn't worry about, or what. But anyway, the symbolic erasure of the trauma would mean the erasure of not only me but also of your mother. She didn't have to worry about getting destroyed fifteen years ago, because she'd already committed suicide as part of the process of conjuring the thing. But now you're here. And like I was saying before, according to the mystical logic of the creature, your flesh and your mother's is the same thing."

"Bullshit," spat Carol.

Snake spoke up: "Maybe let's keep on the safe side, hon."

"Anyway," Harold said, "kill me, and who will explain to you about your dreams?"

"You don't know shit about my dreams. You're just guessing, making up reasons to be useful. I hired an assassin to track you down on behalf of my mother, so it's not hard to guess that maybe I've been dreaming about her lately."

Harold shook his head. "Nah," he said. "These dreams are special."

Earlier, mere moments earlier, he'd been scared of her. Now he seemed smug, like he had her number and knew what she was and wasn't capable of. It infuriated her all over again, and added another stone to the burden of her many failures as a daughter. She began to shake, and she told herself that if it looked like she was going to cry then before that could happen she would jump on Harold and kill him with her bare hands. "I ought to stab you through your fucking heart," she said. "And before I come down off this hill, I'm going to."

He shook his head again. "No. You want to be the good guy. Well, you can't be the good guy and also rip up the people you hate, even if we deserve it. Believe me, you don't get to have everything."

Snake moseyed over and nudged Harold with the barrel of her rifle. "Hey," she said. "Just FYI: I don't want to be a good guy. What I want is to stay alive and make money. And I *am* going to get to have that."

24

Four

The next bit of Snake's spiel was that Harold was going to help her accomplish those two goals, if he felt like staying alive. But he protested that he needed rest—he began slurring his words and couldn't keep his eyes open even to focus on the gun in his face. So Snake decided he wasn't bullshitting when he said that tossing up that force-field had taken strength which he absolutely had to replenish, and she agreed to let him curl up on the dirt floor and sleep.

"You sleep, too," she told Carol. "I'll stay up and keep watch."

"All right," said Carol, even though she felt too wired, frightened, sad, and angry to sleep. "What about you, though? I guess you'll wake me up in a couple hours so I can take a shift?"

But Snake shook her head. "I'm good for another day," she said, like it was nothing.

Carol didn't argue—the weight of everything hit her all at once. She lay on the floor, wrapping herself in a big blanket Snake had found folded up on one of the shelves (hopefully it wasn't cursed or anything). Outside the creature roared again. It didn't sound far away enough for comfort, but at least it seemed to be wandering steadily further away from the cabin site. The distant sound of tearing and crashing wood was constant.

Just before she drifted off, she heard Snake musing to herself: "You know, aside from trying to kill me, that thing out there is pretty boss."

Carol's last conscious thought of the day was that she ought to feel guilty for how glad she was that that thing ensouled by her mom was moving away from them....

Her last conscious thought, in the sense that the next one came after she was asleep. But she was conscious, really. Conscious that she was dreaming, anyway.

She always recognized these dreams. They were always different, but she always recognized them.

In this dream, she woke up in a sort of place she had never actually been. She was in a very soft bed with frilly white sheets; but it was too small for her, and she could feel her feet hanging over the edge.

Sitting up, she looked down at herself: a lacy white princess dress belted with a pink satin sash. She scanned the room: a white, plush, thick carpet; the walls were white, with gold and baby-blue moldings; a white-and-gold armoire; a white-and-gold vanity table, with a little white chair. Over in her peripheral vision, a full-length standing mirror; dimly she registered that there was something funny about it, that made her not want to look at it directly. There were a couple of windows, and white light poured through their gauzy curtains. Somehow Carol knew that if she looked behind those curtains, there would be nothing outside to see. No landscape, no sky. Just the light.

It wasn't just the bed. Everything here was a little small for her. As if the room had been intended for the little girl she'd once been.

She stood up. Her head nearly brushed the ceiling. She looked around (but her eyes just so happened to miss the mirror). There was no door.

"Mom?" she said. As usual, no answer. And as usual, she tried again: "Momma?"

She took a step. The carpet was so thick and lush that it was like moving her feet through cool clear mud. She looked down past her poofy flouncy skirt at her feet in their pink ballet slippers.

"Mom? I never had a room like this, or this kind of shoes. But I secretly wanted it. Is that why you're putting me here, now? I was always afraid to let you find out I wanted stuff like this, because I was embarrassed. But did you actually know, all along?"

She turned this way and that, looking all around the room (yet never quite catching sight of the mirror). It felt as if there were whispering tingles floating at the edges of her awareness, as if a light were flashing at a wavelength just outside the human visual spectrum, as if there were a hum just below the lowest audible pitch.

A hum—but a sentient hum. Maybe a soul was nothing but a vibration.

"Is that you?" she said. She'd meant to call out, but her voice was hushed. "Mom, is that you?"

No answer. Carol would have to guess whether it was her mom or not.

She took another step. *There's no reason for me to be scared, just because there's no door,* she reassured herself. "You wouldn't put me somewhere where I'd get hurt." Aloud, her voice retained that tone of reassurance. Who was she reassuring? Herself? Her mother?

"That thing had your face, Momma," she said, to the ceiling, to the window. "Is it you? Is it kinda-sorta you? If it's you then I know I don't have to be scared. I know that you would never hurt me. Not really."

She winced to hear her own pathetic voice. She recognized her tone, from times when she was a kid, when her mom would get mad at her for no reason and Carol would be the one who'd feel guilty, as if she'd betrayed her mom simply by noticing her injustice, her irrationality. Then she would always come hopping along afterward, talking to her mother in that pollyannaish sing-song, as if nothing bad had happened and she couldn't even remember anything bad ever having happened in her life, as if pretending that was true would defuse her mother's temper.

It had never worked, yet here she was doing it again.

She continued to look around the room, hunting for something that might trigger a brainstorm and help her figure out a way to coax her mother back out into the open. Her eye fell upon the mirror.

It was a fancy mirror with a gilded rocaille trimming, like something you might see at Versailles. (Not that Carol had ever been to Versailles—she'd never gotten to go anywhere.) For a second Carol couldn't put her finger on what was so weird about it. Then she realized that she couldn't see her reflection. Instead she saw something different.

Churning black smoke filled the frame. It was pumping up from bottom to top, scrolling up the glass like sped-up film of factory smoke.

If Carol had seen such a thing while awake, she would have assumed that what was in the mirror frame wasn't a mirror at all, but a computer monitor or something like that. But in this world of dream logic, she knew perfectly well that it was a mirror and that it was showing her something that was really there.

Not an ordinary mirror, though. Carol thought it probably was like the mirror in *Through the Looking-Glass*, and that she was looking at something that lived on its other side.

She took a step closer. She couldn't have said how she sensed it, but somehow she did sense the surface of the mirror vibrating. Like at any moment it might just hum its way out of existence. Once that happened, would the black smoke be free to roil into the room?

Carol took a tentative step toward it.

"Mom?" she said, uncertain.

The black smoke continued to churn. There seemed to be an endless supply. Carol took another half a step. "Mom, are you in there? Is that you?"

It was always like this. She could call to her mom all she wanted, but it was always she who had to go to her mother, never the other way around. "Mom?" she said again.

The surface of the mirror rippled, she thought, as if it were affected by the image it projected, as if its two-dimensional nature were being compromised. Carol held up her hand. She held it out towards the mirror surface.

What would happen if she touched it? She wondered if her hand would pass through, as if through the skin of water, and she wondered if whatever was inside was going to grab her and pull her all the way in....

Carol shot up with a gasp and remembered that her mother was dead.

She didn't remember right away where she was, though. The dim cellar was alien, and the two figures looking at her were strangers. Once she remembered who they were, the knowledge didn't particularly comfort her.

Snake rolled her shoulders and rotated her head, working out some kinks. "Hope you slept good," she said. "I got a little tired after all, and nearly woke you up to take a watch." She sounded cheerful enough, though. "I especially would have done it if I'd realized I was going to be running around, risking getting eaten alive." Carol wondered what she was talking about.

Harold was studying Carol, a funny look on his face. He wore a brown T-shirt and jeans and shoes, instead of the white T-shirt and blue boxers from yesterday—he must have had a change of clothes stashed here. "You wouldn't have been able to wake her," he told Snake. "That wasn't sleep, that was a trance. You had a vision, didn't you?"

Snake looked at Carol to see if she would answer, and when she didn't she took her pistol out to re-check that it was loaded. "You woke up just in time for the fun. Looks like I get to go play tag with the critter."

"You won't be able to stop it," murmured Carol.

Snake and Harold both looked at her again. "Oh, yeah?" said Snake.

"Only I can stop it."

But then she shook her head, as if snapping herself out of something. And when Snake and Harold asked her what she'd meant, she could only tell them to never mind her, that she must still be dreaming.

Five

After she'd recovered from her dream, Carol noticed that Harold was still flushed and sweaty this morning. He looked feverish. Her first reaction was to feel concern, the way she would for any fellow human; this triggered a quiet rage of shame and self-loathing, as if she'd let herself fall for a stupid trick *again*. She wasn't supposed to be giving this prick the benefit of her sympathy, she was supposed to be avenging her mom.

To put some distance between her and him, she forced herself upright and moved back among the shelves, checking stuff out the way Snake had the night before. Out of the corner of her eye she noted with satisfaction Harold's nervousness as he watched her go. Clearing his throat, he called after her, "Ah, you're free to look around, but I'd recommend not to touch anything."

Pointedly, she ignored him. She was very tempted to touch something, just to goad him. Then again, that really might not be a good idea.

Snake said to Harold, "All right—go on with what you were saying."

Harold went back to outlining his crazy-sounding plan for subduing the monster.

It wasn't a complicated plan, and five minutes later Harold had explained the whole thing, complete with a crude map of the clearing which he'd traced in the dirt floor. Snake was dubious. She pointed to the little square Harold had drawn, which was near the big square that represented his fallen house, on the other side of it from the X that marked the cellar they were in now. "So this is the shed where I find your little thingamajig. Is it gonna be easy? Is the thing just gonna pop out at me?"

"Well…. You might have to do some poking around. I've accumulated a lot of stuff over the years."

"Great. So what's this prayer wheel look like?"

"They usually look like pinwheels, I think," said Carol, stepping out from the shelves. Nodding at Harold, she said, "How come you don't go after it, instead of Snake? You're the one who knows what the thing looks like and exactly where it is."

"I actually don't remember *exactly* where it is—I haven't been in that shed for years, it's kind of a mess. And if either you or I leave the screen of this Refuge, the creature will sense us at once. It's already costing me an effort to camouflage us, even with the aid of this Refuge's built-in cloaking spells."

That explained his sheen of sweat, Carol supposed.

Snake said, "The critter'll see you and Carol. But I'm, what? Invisible?"

"No. But the creature will be able to sense you only with its mundane senses, the same as any animal. Sight, smell, hearing. If you can manage not to attract its attention, you'll be fine."

"And if I can't manage?"

"It'll try to kill you."

"Uh-huh. Say that happens, and I can't get back here. Any other hidey-holes? I'm starting to get the feeling you've got a whole little compound set up here. Why don't you draw me a nice detailed map of the whole set-up."

Harold's mouth twisted, like he'd tasted something bad. It burned Carol up. He didn't deserve the luxury of getting to deem things unpleasant. "I'd rather not," he said.

Snake took her handgun out of its holster and held it to his head. "For the sake of argument, say I'm gonna blow your brains out if you don't."

That sparked a flurry of blinking from Harold. His voice wavered as he said, "You would never know whether or not I was lying."

Snake put the gun away. "Yeah, I guess you're right. Anyway. This thing looks like a pinwheel? Is the kid right about that?"

"It's not a pinwheel. It's much more involved than that. But, yes, that is basically what it looks like."

"Okey-dokey." She pored over the map in the dirt, and started to look dubious again. "So what happened to this coven that helped you out last time?" she asked. "Can't you just get your witch girlfriend on the horn to tell her you need another favor? Maybe get us some back-up?"

"She passed away," said Harold.

From his tone, it sounded like an old grief whose early bitterness had smoothed away. Carol took the risk of being nosey and gently asked, "Was she sick?"

"No. Her whole coven got taken out by a team of paramilitary Jesuits." A moment passed before he realized that both women were staring at him. "There's, like, this whole scene that you guys don't really know anything about," he explained.

Snake checked the magazine in the AR-15. Other than that, her final preparations consisted only of raising her arms overhead for a big stretch, then touching her toes a few times. Before she left she walked over to Carol and held out to her the smaller of her two handguns. "Here," she said. "In case your playmate Harold gets frisky and needs a time-out."

Carol shrank from the firearm. "I don't even know how to use those things."

"You point the end with the hole at the guy you want to shoot and squeeze the trigger. Just like in the movies, more or less."

Carol shook her head. "No, thanks."

"Honey, I like you. You're the special-needs daughter I never had. That's why I'm gonna take the time to explain this. When your muscle has to leave you alone with a rapist who knows you've hired someone to assassinate him, it's best to be armed."

When Snake put it that way, Carol had to acknowledge that it did seem reasonable. Sheepishly she took the gun.

Snake climbed the wooden ladder up to the trapdoor. Slowly she lifted it and blinked in the daylight. She looked around, but saw no sign of the creature—then she heard the crackling of broken underbrush. The noise came from the other side of the shattered pile of wood that had been the front half of the cabin, so Snake figured she had a brief window in which to get away from the Refuge. Even if she wound up being spotted, there was no sense leading the creature to her client.

The nearest cover was the ruins of the cabin, so even though that was close to the monster Snake scrambled over to it.

Crouching behind a pile of broken wood, she listened to the monster. It was so big that it would have been impossible not to hear it as it moved through the dry foliage; but Snake's hearing was naturally sharp and she had trained it to be sharper still, so she could go one better and tell that the monster was moving away from her.

Snake knew that the thing was not simply a big animal, but it was more like a big animal than it was like anything else in her experience. And no big animal she had ever heard of would walk backwards through the woods.

So if it was moving away from her she could bet it wasn't looking toward her. That meant she ought to be able to make a dash for the shed, more or less safely, if she took off running right now. She could see the little building up ahead.

Her leg muscles quivered with anticipation as she prepared to bolt. But something held her back. Not fear. She listened closely to the noises coming from the creature. It was breathing hard: huffing, sighing. She remembered the sight of it the night before, the way she'd been able to see through it, the way it hadn't been solid, exactly, even though it had clearly been capable of wreaking some pretty solid havoc. Why did an ectoplasmic creature that wasn't a hundred percent existent on the physical plane need to breathe, she wondered?

What she should be doing was sprinting her ass over to that shed and nabbing that pinwheel the target wanted, so he could send the big girl back to the phantom zone.

But Snake found that what she really wanted to do was just *look* at her.

She stood, slowly, and poked her head up from behind the pile of broken timber.

Sure enough, there was the creature, nosing through the woods, not far from the spot where she and the kid had been hiding when Harold sprang out of the cabin yesterday.

It was big, all right. About the size of an elephant, Snake reckoned. But not particularly threatening at the moment. For one thing, it remained partly see-through, and its cool blue luminosity seemed less impressive in the sunlight than it had at dusk. Friendly, almost. For another, even though Snake didn't think it was actually eating leaves or anything, seeing it nose around in the vegetation that way made it look like some kind of big herbivore. It was hard for Snake to be scared of a plant-eater, though she would be sensibly cautious around it.

The truth was, she thought it was cute.

Even from this distance, Snake's sharp eyes could see that while some of the leaves and twigs seemed to pass right through the monster's ectoplasmic manifestation or whatever, others were pushed out of the way or snapped off, just as they would be by a normal animal. Snake wondered why sometimes the thing interacted with the physical world and sometimes it didn't. It seemed to her that anything that interacted with the physical world ought to be subject to physical control, if she could just figure out the means.

Standing there gazing at it, she let herself drift into a reverie. That was uncharacteristically careless of her. Then the monster suddenly turned that long prehensile neck to gaze over its shoulder with that weirdly humanoid face.

Now that it was looking at her, the thing no longer seemed like some leaf-munching gentle giant. It let out a cloudsplitting shriek with that vicious fucking face it had, and turned and charged at Snake.

Snake darted for the shed. She knew that no two-legged animal had much chance of outrunning a multi-legged one, but she had a big head start and she was racing across the more or less level top of the hill, while the monster was gathering steam up the slope. She would be able to make it to the shed; as for getting back to the cellar, or Refuge, or whatever, she'd have to figure that out when the time came. In about ten seconds.

She threw open the shed door. She'd hoped to have time to grab the pinwheel before dealing with the monster, but a quick glance told her Harold hadn't been kidding: this shed was a sty. Where was the pinwheel in this jumble of crap?! A crate of coconuts caught her eye. Why the hell did Harold have those?

She spun around and began firing her rifle into the creature seconds before it ran her down.

As she squeezed the trigger, she had no idea whether the bullets would have any effect on the big girl at all, as they had last night, or whether they would just pass through her like smoke.

A bit of both. She could see the traces bursting from her gun; and then she could see them after they penetrated the monster's "skin"—they slowed down massively, as if they were traveling through some region where time moved differently, and they left behind them ripples of a thicker, more opaque, more luminous blue.

The bullets didn't rip the creature apart, the way they would have done to something made of flesh. But the big girl did feel them. She reared back on her hind legs and kicked her forelegs into the air (she had two forelegs—at the moment she had three legs in the back, but it kept changing), and let out another bone-shattering shriek.

In its agony, the monster seemed to have slowed down— like the whole creature was enveloped in mystical molasses; its shrieking head rocked back and forth too slowly, its forelegs kicked in slow motion, gravity took its time pulling the beast back to earth, and its shriek's pitch deepened steadily, sloping down and down and down.

That bought Snake a few seconds to stick her face back in the junk shed. If she didn't see that fucking pinwheel in the next two seconds, she wasn't exactly in a position to root around for it.

She did see it, though. Must have been focused by the pressure. Or else just lucky.

Assuming this really was the right doohickey. It looked right, anyway, a wooden stick with a wheel of pinkish paper fans attached, sitting atop a stack of dusty wooden crates.

She took off running even as she grabbed it. The monster was falling to earth as she darted around it—despite moving in slow-motion it still rattled the ground when it hit, and started shrieking again as Snake ran past, unloading her rifle at it as she went.

The gunfire slowed the big girl down again, but not as drastically. Maybe she was getting used to it. After a brief delay, Snake heard the thing hauling ass after her. It sounded like the creature was moving relatively slowly, but maybe not slowly enough.

It might have been Snake's imagination, but she thought it sounded like the monster was picking up speed. Certainly the next scream sounded pretty close.

Snake considered pausing to spin around and shoot some more, but the big girl would almost certainly run her down. Besides, she was nearly at the cellar. She could see its wooden trapdoor up ahead. Only seconds away.

"Hey!" she screamed. "Open up!" There would be good reasons for them to ignore her—unsealing their little Refuge while the monster was so near might risk letting the thing in. On the other hand, Snake was clenching the pinwheel in her fist, and supposedly they needed that if they wanted to get rid of this bitch.

And besides, Snake bet the kid would open up for her. She had a good feeling about that kid.

"The fucking door!" she screamed, almost upon it. Right at her back she could hear the monster's huffing and snarls, could hear and feel her thundering pace. There wasn't going to be time for her to open the door herself.

Just before she was on top of it the hatch popped open. Snake jumped in feet-first, with no time to check if anyone was under her. Overhead she heard a roar and a whoosh. No sooner did she land in a crouch than she had her gun pointing straight back up at the hatch, expecting to see the monster trying to force her way through the narrow hole, or at least sending her snaky head down to try to fucking bite everyone. But instead she saw Harold up on the ladder, pulling the door closed and latching it.

He jumped a little when he looked down and saw the rifle pointing his way. "We're safe again," he assured her. "The conjuration doesn't know the Refuge is here. It can't sense this place at all."

"What is there to sense? She just saw me duck in here."

"From the conjuration's point of view, you simply disappeared. If it tries to remember what it saw—which would be a tall order, because it doesn't have much of a mind—then its memories will be muddled and unclear. If it tries to retrace its steps back to where it saw you wink out, then it will find itself strangely unable to do so. Even trying to think about it will be exhausting, and since the conjuration lacks mental stamina, it'll give up soon enough."

"Okay, you're the warlock, so whatever you say. I got your magic pinwheel. Doesn't look like it got damaged."

"It's *not* a pinwheel," Harold said, snatching it from her. Gently snatching it, if such a thing were possible. He really was offended, and she thought about telling him that before he got all hoity-toity he might want to remember who had all the guns and had been hired to kill him. But fuck it, she decided. Better to keep your mouth shut and listen and learn; this guy knew a bunch of shit worth knowing.

"How did you get away from that thing?" asked Carol.

"You didn't throw any of my Gourds at her, did you?" asked Harold.

"No. I used my gun. What gourds?"

"Ctholian Gourds of Submission. They look like coconuts— there are a few in the shed, and after you left it occurred to me that I ought to have told you to be on the lookout for them, because they probably would have weakened the conjuration. But anyway, I'm glad it wasn't necessary. Those are hard to get."

Harold held the pinwheel carefully, as if it were made of glass (it *was* made of old wood and dry paper, which Snake supposed was even more delicate), and turned to Carol. "All right," he said. "We've got the prayer wheel, so the plan is on. We'll practice today, and then go forward before sunset."

Carol didn't look thrilled. "I don't know if I even believe any of this," she protested. "I mean, why the hell should I believe you about *anything?*"

"Because I want to survive." From his firm tone, you wouldn't have guessed that he was talking to a woman who had hired a bounty hunter to tie him up and torture him to death. "If that's going to happen, if the plan is going to work, then you're going to have to believe me. More important, you're going to have to believe in *yourself.*"

"You know, talking like a cheap-ass motivational speaker does not make your plan sound any less stupid."

"Hey," Snake barked, putting an end to their squabble before it could really get underway. They looked at her, startled. "I'm the one who risked her life getting this pinwheel," she reminded them. "So the plan had *better* fucking work."

Both of them looked so abashed, it was funny. Like kids. Even so, Harold couldn't stop himself from muttering a barely audible protest under his breath: "It's not a *pinwheel,*" he said.

Six

Ten minutes earlier, after Harold had shut the trapdoor once Snake had shimmied herself up out of it to go get the prayer wheel, he had turned to face Carol. She was holding Snake's gun on him with a stance she'd picked up from cop shows: feet wide apart, right hand holding the gun and her left hand holding her right wrist to stabilize it, both hands out ramrod-straight before her. Suddenly self-conscious that she was aping all these stupid TV shows, she almost relaxed her body. But then she reflected that it wasn't as if she knew of a better way to point a gun at somebody. Maybe the way they did it on TV was right.

Harold watched her carefully. "You look like you really are about to shoot me," he observed.

"Yeah, well, that was the whole point of coming out here," she said, trying to sound like a hard-ass, even though she wasn't planning to shoot and had only meant to cover him.

"I thought the whole reason you came here was to have *her* do it," he said, nodding up at the door Snake had just gone through.

Wrong thing to say. Shame bubbled up her spine and into her guts and chest cavity, the shame of not being a good enough daughter. She jabbed the gun at him, and something in her face made him take a quick step back and raise his hands.

"She only came along to help make sure I *did* get you," Carol growled. "And now I have."

Without lowering his hands, he pointed at the trapdoor and said, "That conjuration out there has got both of us. We need each other if we're going to live. I need you, and you need me."

41

"I'm not sure I even should live. Is me dying such a big price to pay for letting my mom get the revenge she wanted? Would a good daughter get in her way? And what happens after we do die? Does the monster just fade out? That would let Snake get away, at least. Why should Snake have to get killed for the sake of our drama?"

Harold stared at her. "What? Why should *you* die? What are you talking about? Listen, I told you, that thing out there is not your mother...."

"What you told me was that my mother created it out of her soul or essence or whatever...."

"As the raw material, yes, but in and of itself *that thing is not your mother*. It's a tool she created. It's true her reason for creating it was to kill me, but I'm sure she would have thought twice if she'd known it would also mean killing *you*."

Carol didn't say anything; she wasn't so sure her mother wouldn't have let her die, if that had been what it took. Even entertaining an idea like that for a moment, even involuntarily, made her feel guilty.

Harold continued: "Besides, even if there were no question of you getting caught in the crossfire, even if you could just unleash that thing and know it wouldn't do damage to anyone but me, then I should still point out that your mom was not exactly her best self when she conjured it to go out and kill me."

Carol forced out a bitter, mirthless laugh. "Oh, yeah? How would you know? What is it that came along and turned my mom into this less-than-best self?"

Hands still up, Harold shrugged. "Me. I came along. She trusted me, and I raped her. You know that. Afterward she was fucked up, because that kind of experience does fuck you up. I assume she stayed fucked up right through your childhood, since she died by committing suicide so as to summon a conjuration. One of the really tragic consequences of what I did is that you never got to meet the Theresa I knew, when I first encountered her. You know, when that conjuration first came for me, fifteen years ago, that was the first time it really came home to me, what I'd done."

The gun was quivering in Carol's hands. "This is not a topic you want to continue with, dickface," she growled.

Hesitantly, Harold lowered his hands a couple inches. "Carol, are you truly going to shoot me?"

"I am absolutely going to retain the motherfucking option."

Harold slowly lowered his hands down to his sides. He said, "You don't want to go down that road. Believe me. Take it from a guy who's been to some pretty dark places."

"I'm going to send you to the darkest place of all if you don't stop giving me lectures."

But, although he remained cautious, she could tell he didn't really buy it anymore. He was calling her bluff. And it was no good. She might have been able to muster the willpower to sit through it while someone else killed him. But right at this moment she didn't have it in her to shoot him in cold blood.

Even if he did think she was unlikely to shoot him, he kept his hands visible and didn't step any closer. "I was already changing fifteen years ago," he said, "when the conjuration first appeared. I was already on my way to becoming a different person, but dealing with that thing out there, realizing what your mother must have had to do in order to summon it, understanding just how much pain I must have caused her, all that finished the job. In a way your mom succeeded in her purpose. The man who did those terrible things to her is dead. What's left of me is only a shadow. But a shadow with no interest in hurting anyone, at least."

"Bullshit."

"You don't believe people can change? You don't believe people have untapped potentials within them? I hope you change your mind about that, Carol, I really do. Because we're going to need to unlock *your* potential, if we're going to beat that thing. I see so much of your mother in you."

"Dude, shut the fuck up about my mother."

He took a half-step forward. "It's true," he said. "Goddam, but your mom was a powerful witch. I remember the first time I saw her, at a sort of a, uh ... a gathering, in upstate New York. It was like she'd swallowed a star and its glow was leaking out from all her pores. There were some pretty potent people there, but she put them all to shame. And I'm telling you, I see that same power now in you."

"You're trying to con me," she said, with the tired familiar bitterness one reserves for an old disappointment. "I've never been able to do any of the stuff that Mom could do."

"Because you've never had a teacher. A guide. Now, I know that, for reasons which are painfully obvious, I'm not much of a pick to be your guru...."

"You have got to be fucking kidding me...."

"If that conjuration weren't prowling around outside, I would give you some names and telephone numbers. Of people who'd be more equipped to lead you to the power that awaits inside you. Assuming we survive, I'll do that. But first we do have to survive. And the only way is if you listen to me, because we're going to need your power. I'm not strong enough to take that thing on my own. Fifteen years ago my friends and I were only able to send it hibernating in the ether—it must have started to stir, and that's why you began having the dreams. But I'm willing to bet that you, with your flesh-and-blood link to its creator, can destroy it for good."

"If we survive, I'm going to kill you."

"Is that really what you want? I saw your face last night, when I was tied up and gagged. Isn't there a part of you that was relieved when the conjuration showed up, relieved that you didn't have to go through with it? Not being a killer is nothing to be ashamed of, you know. And you don't have to let me off scott-free. Once this is all over you can have your friend march me down to the nearest police station, and I'll confess."

"The statute of limitations has run out, asswipe."

"But I'll still confess." His eyes got wet and his voice thickened. "I'll go on the record for what I did. I'll do it at the police station. I'll write out a confession, buy ad space in a newspaper, and have it printed, if you like. That's what you really want, isn't it? Isn't what drives you crazy the idea of me walking around in the world, being able to shake people's hands and look them in the eye without their ever realizing I'm a scumbag?"

Carol didn't reply right away.

She hated to admit it, but she did want to live.

Around that time they heard gunfire and then Snake screaming for them to open the door. Once Snake had handed over the prayer wheel, Carol made him outline the plan again, while Snake dusted herself off and took a stroll among Harold's dusty shelves.

Carol was dubious. "That just doesn't sound like a very impressive action, considering how big that creature is."

"That's because *we* are not really doing much. All we're going is using the Tuvokian prayer wheel to summon the spirits of Tuvok and beg their intercession. If it works, it'll weaken the conjuration. And the conjuration should finally grow so weak that it winks out of existence."

She didn't even bother asking who Tuvok was or why he had spirits floating around in the vicinity. Apparently part of the reason Harold had picked this site was that the whole area was sprinkled with mystical convergences, supernatural beings, concentrated magical nodes, stuff like that.

"But so the conjuration's just going to come back in fifteen years or whatever?"

"No. Not this time. All the coven could do was force it into a sort of hibernation—true, a hibernation that might have gone on forever if we hadn't come into contact, but still, something far short of annihilation. But because you're of the same flesh and blood as the original spellcaster, you *do* have the power to annihilate it. It's primarily your power that the Tuvokian spirits are going to use. They know how to draw it from you. Mystically speaking, the duel is between the you and the conjuration. Because mystically speaking, you're one and the same."

Carol frowned. "But the conjuration is not my mom, though."

"No, no, no, no, no. It's formed from the *substance* of your mother. But it is an 'it.' No more your mother, than your fingernail clippings are 'you.' Or, well, a more appropriate analogy would be your excrement, to be quite frank."

"Hey, warlock," called Snake from within the rows of shelves. "Any way you could throw some sort of magical leash on her?"

Harold frowned. "Theoretically, if it were much much weaker than it is. But it's safer to get rid of it."

"Sure, but it might be more *profitable* to keep it available. Under control. Like, maybe we could figure out a way to feed and water and train it. Would sure make my life easier if I could bring that girl along on gigs." She was looking at a crate of coconuts, like she'd seen before in the shed. Must be more of Harold's Gourds of Submission. She made a note.

Harold gasped and his jaw dropped. He stalked angrily through the bunker to Snake; since he was still gripping the prayer wheel, which really did look like a primitive toy, it was a funny sight. Like a little boy taking himself seriously.

He rounded the corner on Snake and started in on her, without noticing the gourds she'd been studying: "We cannot *monetize* this thing! Or *weaponize* it!"

She regarded his distress with her usual cool amusement. "She already looks pretty weaponized to me, man."

"It's not a 'she,' it's an 'it'! Try to remember that you don't know what the hell you're talking about!"

She tilted her head at a subtle warning angle, and there was an ever so slight shift in the quality of her smile. "And you try to remember that I'm still under contract to slowly disassemble you with pliers. Okay, warlock? I just was curious as to whether it was possible to control her. And you just said that it is."

He fumed a moment longer, fury and terror duking it out within him. "I'm not a warlock, I'm a *mage*," he muttered.

Carol listened to their exchange. The pulverization of the cabin wall still vibrated in her mind. Could they risk taking the conjuration out into the world? She had a vision of it getting out of control, going on a rampage, and destroying more houses. Only in her vision, the houses it destroyed weren't isolated cabins inhabited by craven rapists, but suburban houses, filled with mothers, fathers, and daughters.

She stepped past cowed, angry, quivering Harold. Snake watched her approach with light interest.

"I know you've always been the toughest person in the room," Carol said. "But that conjuration, or whatever it's called, isn't a person. You can't control it."

"You don't know the rooms I've been in," Snake observed. "I've had the chance to learn my limits, believe you me."

"Then who knows, maybe you could control that thing," said Carol, not believing it for a second. "But it's my...." She had to pause to clear her throat, then continued: "But that thing is somehow tied up with my mother. So I can't.... I mean, obviously it isn't my mother, I know that. But I can't stand the thought of it running around out there. Because of.... Because it should just be laid to rest, I feel like."

Snake kept studying her. So little of the usual amusement remained visible in her face that it was almost as if there were none there at all. Finally, she said, "Okay. I hear you."

"Great." Carol didn't know why she should suddenly feel so good. It was almost like the feeling when one makes a pass at a boy who's out of one's league and he goes for it. "That's great, thanks."

Realizing that at least part of her elation was at feeling herself taken seriously by Snake, she laughed silently. *I get to sit at the big table and talk to the grown-ups.*

She and Harold spent the next hour going over his plan again and again. "You will spin the prayer wheel," he said, forming each syllable with that careful monotone people adopt when they are repeating something for the third time. "You must do it at a slow, steady, constant rate. You must turn the wheel by lightly grasping the fan blades with the thumb and forefinger of your left hand, while holding the wheel with your right. As you spin the wheel, you must chant, in the Tuvokian Supplicatory Tongue. I will feed you this chant—I will say the words, and you will repeat them. Each syllable must be repeated exactly as I say it—butchering the Tuvokian Supplicatory Tongue will offend the Tuvokian spirits, and we'll be screwed. Don't forget that all this while you must be turning the prayer wheel, in exactly the way that I described."

As he talked Carol stared at him like he was crazy. "And us turning this prayer wheel and saying this chant I don't even understand will bring that creature under control?"

"Yes," said Harold, his voice frayed since he was repeating this answer for the fourth time. "And if we mess it up the spirits will be offended and they'll leave and we'll be in big trouble. There are other spirits dwelling within this clearing, but they're even less pliable than the Tuvokians. In order for the Tuvokian spirits to have access at all to the conjuration, I have to lower the Refuge's defenses. That means it's going to sense us, and come running. If we aren't chanting the right way when it comes, then we're goners. It'll have us cornered in here."

"Well, let's rehearse, then," said Carol.

"No! Jesus! It's not a wedding dinner! Once we start, *that's it*. The ritual will have begun! We only get to do it once. If we start it before we're ready, we're screwed!"

Carol was getting more and more freaked out. "Well, if precision is so important, how come *you* don't spin the wheel and say the chant? You're the one who knows what he's doing!"

"Yes, but you're the one with the power, Carol. I know you don't believe me, because you don't feel it. But that's because you've never been guided. It does reside in you, though. I can sense it, and as long as you go through the motions I tell you, the power will flow out of you and will add the needed force. It'll just happen—you won't need to think about it, any more than you need to think about firing your synapses when you decide to raise your arm. And the Tuvokians will see that power, and will know how to borrow its force for their battle with the conjuration."

Snake interrupted them. "Why don't we get the drop on the thing? Instead of waiting around here?" she asked. "Why don't

48

we go out into the woods and sneak up on her? You can guide us through your little obstacle course."

Harold was exasperated. "Don't you understand? If Carol and I leave the Refuge, the conjuration will immediately sense us. Not you, but Carol and me. Besides, I don't know my way around all those booby traps. If I go into the woods to hunt squirrels or something, I stick to a few patches that I know are safe."

"What? You don't know where the traps are? Didn't you set all this up?"

"Yes. But it was fifteen years ago, and I did it over the course of a single night, with power I'd borrowed from my friend's coven. It was the last big spell I ever cast. I mean, obviously these physical booby traps wouldn't do much good against the conjuration, but I, er, made plenty of other, corporeal enemies in my day. The booby traps are mainly for them.... Anyway, for years I avoided going far into the woods, to be safe instead of sorry. And now I don't even know where the traps are anymore."

Carol laughed. "The traps keep folks out, but they also keep you in. You're like a minotaur. A middle-aged, balding minotaur."

"Well, regardless of whether you know where the traps are or not, I can spot 'em," said Snake.

Snake left them alone with their preparations. Even if they couldn't practice with the actual prayer wheel, Carol insisted on practicing with *something*—the pressure was too great otherwise. Rummaging around, Harold scrounged up something that looked a lot like the Tuvokian prayer wheel, but apparently really was nothing but a pinwheel. Carol sat with him, painstakingly turning it by gripping the blades with the thumb and middle finger of her left hand. He strictly vetoed her plea that they practice the Tuvokian chant, though—he even looked over his shoulder as if the Tuvokians might be within earshot, and offended that anyone would suggest being so cavalier with their language.

As she spun the wheel, she looked at him dubiously. "It's not that I don't believe in magic," she said. "I mean, obviously that thing out there is magical. Plus it's not like I didn't see my mom move stuff with her mind and all that, when I was growing up. But this whole thing about how I have some sort of mystical essence inside me, that's just going to automatically kick in if I spin this wheel and chant these words … I don't know...."

"It's a bridge too far?" suggested Harold, understandingly.

"I guess so, yeah," she said, almost grateful. So great was her need for guidance and reassurances from someone who knew what was what, that for the moment she didn't even notice that she wasn't thinking about revenge, that she was instead looking at him like he was that guru he had so accurately declared himself unfit to be.

Harold nodded. "I get it. But it's true. That power is there within you—the wheel and the chant are just ways to access it. Because they're primitive ways, they can't access a lot of it—but it should be enough."

"Are you sure? I mean, that thing outside is no joke."

"Oh, I'm sure," he said, and she could tell that he wasn't just pep-talking her, that he really meant it. "I've been trained to see it. You can't because you haven't been, even though it's there within yourself. But you'll be able to find a *real* teacher, once we get out of here."

Then his smile faded and he got a wistful, then a pained look. In a faraway voice he said, "Really, it would have been best if your mother could have given you some guidance, from your childhood on. But I guess...." He trailed off.

Carol forgot to practice turning the pinwheel at the same time she remembered to be angry. But it was a confused anger. Not doubtful; she had no doubt that she should be angry at Harold. He was so different from what she'd expected, though. And her duty to hurt him kept being jostled aside by her need to comprehend.

With a bitter scowl (almost, strangely, a betrayed one), she said, "So how come you did it? Raped my mom?" As she pushed the word "raped" out of her mouth she tried to make it sound as ugly as she could, yet when she heard it, it didn't seem ugly enough.

Harold looked at her, startled. "Power," he said, as if he'd thought that was obvious, as if he'd assumed she'd already known. "I told you, your mother was filled with power, she shone with it. Female power. And I got into some pretty dark stuff as a young mage. Some black roads, some demonic alliances. Some of the things I did, the kinds of power I wanted to achieve, they sometimes required sacrifice. For example, the violation of a strong woman. I grabbed at cheap power and selfish gratification when I was young, and I've been paying for it ever since.... I mean, that doesn't excuse anything, obviously."

"No. Obviously."

"I'm just telling you the way it was and how it happened. Painful as it is, I assume part of the reason you came here was to learn that, in addition to killing me."

He waited. Carol didn't say anything. She avoided looking at him and went back to spinning the practice wheel. He took that as assent and continued.

"I won't lie, it's a thrill, that kind of power. A dark thrill. When I ... well, when I did the deed ... it wasn't the way that sort of thing normally goes down, in case you're interested. It was part of an elaborate ritual, that I had to lure your mother into. But part of the thrill was mundane. Unrelated to magic, to ritual. There was a part of me, a soft part, that I had to burn down and destroy in order to go through with it. And even though that hurt in a way, it was a sort of pleasure-pain. Because I felt like I was making myself stronger, by destroying those soft, gentle parts of my psyche. It was only later on in my life that I realized I hadn't made myself stronger, at all."

Carol didn't reply, just kept turning the pinwheel. Even before, for example when watching "Oprah," she'd always thought there was something grotesquely self-indulgent about criminals giving themselves permission to painstakingly unpack and detail all the psychological motives for their crimes and the mental cost they'd paid for their own weakness, as if the audience were expected to forgive their sins just because the sinners had taken the trouble to analyze themselves; now that the crime being discussed was against her mother, she felt a strong urge to bite Harold's face. But she kept her mouth shut because, after all, he was right—she did want to know.

He cleared his throat, as if now he was about to enter into a delicate subject (which was pretty mind-blowing, when one considered what he'd been talking about up to now). "I don't want to piss you off," he said. "But when I look at you, at what you're doing ... I recognize a bit of who I was back then. Not that it's the same. Not that you don't have justification for what you're doing, and not that I did. But I look at your face, when you tell me the things you're going to do to punish me, or when I'm sure you're thinking about them, and it's like gazing into a time-travel mirror. I see myself, the way I must have looked, when I was killing those soft parts inside me that were telling me not to do what I did. And I'm here to tell you, you can never get that softness back, and you're not stronger without it. It's like I told you yesterday—you don't get to have everything."

It pissed her off that he kept telling her she couldn't have everything. Like she was some kid who didn't already know that. After a deep breath, she looked up at him. He could see the fury in her face; but she could tell that he had expected it, had allowed for it. There was something calculating in his expression, as if he had carefully predicted the effect his words would have upon her and now was weighing the results against those predictions. But that calculation did not necessarily mean he was lying, she pointed out to herself.

Keeping her voice under careful, tight control, she said, "How about this. How about you just stick to teaching me what I need to know."

"Absolutely," he said, still watching her closely, as if she were a danger he needed to be careful of. Which she was. But also as if she were a danger he felt he could handle. "I'll teach you everything you need."

Seven

They could only practice so much. Even if spinning the prayer wheel exactly that way was slightly awkward, it didn't take long to master the technique, and they couldn't rehearse the chant.

But Carol insisted on taking a nap. Snake was dubious; "You just slept all night," she said. But Harold stuck up for her. She hadn't really slept in the normal way, she'd had a vision (he claimed to be able to tell); and having a vision can wear you out.

So Snake relented. Carol curled up in a corner and slept hard for hours. Snake tied Harold up and amused herself with more snooping, now and then bringing something over for Harold to explain or identify.

At last Carol felt someone roughly shaking her, and again there was the panic of not knowing where she was or who with—for a second she didn't even know how old she was, and would have believed she was a child again. Snake's gruff, no-nonsense voice yanked her back to reality: "C'mon, get up. You've been asleep for hours."

Carol struggled to sit up, feeling as heavy and stiff as if her blood had been sand. "Really?" she mumbled. It didn't feel like it. Rolling her shoulders to try to loosen them, she said, "What time is it?"

"Time for you to get a watch. A hair past a freckle. And only about an hour away from nightfall. When you sleep, hon, you don't fuck around. Now let's get this show started before we lose the day."

Carol was shocked. "I slept that long?"

"You were exhausted," put in Harold, untied now. "More exhausted than you know. And you're going to need all your strength for what's coming."

"Wait. I thought all I had to do was spin that wheel and repeat your chant?"

"Right. You won't need much energy for any *physical* activities. Not mental ones either, strictly speaking. But we did need to make sure your metaphysical stores are full, if you see what I mean."

Carol did not see. A shudder passed through her. Still sitting on the ground, she looked back and forth at the two older people looming over her. "And it's really almost nighttime?" What if things went wrong? She imagined that thing on a rampage and her trying to run from it, through those booby-trapped woods in the dark. "Maybe we ought to wait till morning, then."

After all the crazy shit that had gone down, this was the first time Carol ever heard Snake sound truly frustrated. "No, goddammit!" she barked. "All day you've been sleeping, supposedly so that you could do this thing. Now that you've slept all day you want to sit up all night and wait till morning. And then you'll be tuckered out and want to put it off so you can sleep again. No, no, no fucking way."

Under Harold's guidance, Carol took her place: seated cross-legged, her back to the entrance. He sat next to her.

"Just before we begin," he explained, "I'll deactivate the cloaking spell. The Refuge will no longer be very worthy of the name, although even after the conjuration has spotted us there are a few warding spells around the door that should slow it down, and keep it from immediately bursting in here to kill us. Not for long, though."

"Wow, great," said Carol.

"No choice. We can't very well lure it into our sphere of influence if we're cloaked. Don't worry, it'll all be fine, as long as you spin the wheel correctly and repeat the chant in precisely the right way."

No pressure or anything, Carol said to herself sullenly. Harold's manner was lively, and Carol suspected he was getting off on all this. Maybe it had been a long time since he'd gotten to take part in some big magic.

"We sit with our backs to the entrance," Harold explained. "We mustn't turn and look at the conjuration, even after it's broken through the door. Turning our backs to it represents our indifference to and disdain for it. If we show fear, then the fickle Tuvokian spirits will decide we think they can't protect us, and they'll grow offended and abandon our cause."

"Fuck that," said Snake, "I'm keeping an eye on that big bitch."

"You can look at it—you don't matter," said Harold, but not in a tone like he meant anything unpleasant by it. "You have no magic to speak of. Anyway, between the magic pooled together by myself and Carol—mainly Carol—and the fact that we're the conjuration's target, the metaphysical blare will probably drown you out completely. The conjuration may not sense you at all, and probably won't care if it does."

"Sounds fine to me," shrugged Snake. "Let's say you turn out not to know what you're doing and your pinwheel has no effect. Got a Plan B?"

But Harold offered no answer to that question. Except to repeat, in a stubborn little voice, "It's a *prayer* wheel."

He and Carol were sitting cross-legged in the dirt with the prayer wheel and their backs to the door. Carol was secretly praying for a reprieve. Snake sat in front of them, on top of a crate, her AR-15 cradled in her lap and her eyes fixed on the trapdoor. Carol took note of her expression as she stared at the door. There was no fear, and she envied that. It even looked almost like Snake couldn't wait for them to get started. Carol yearned to have that kind of bravery, even if you had to be a little nuts first.

Harold was scared, but he did a pretty good job of hiding it. "Put your thumb and middle finger on one of the blades," he said, the quiver in his voice barely perceptible, "and prepare to begin spinning it, *slowly and steadily*, the moment I begin chanting. At the same time, you must pay extremely close attention to the chant so you can repeat each syllable exactly the right way."

"Dude, I am so fucking scared right now. Are the Tuvokians going to be offended by me showing this fear?"

"Don't worry, I only meant we couldn't show fear in a ritual sense. I'm sure you're going to do fine. Just don't make any mistakes."

"Fucking start!" shouted Snake. It was like their unending delays irritated her more than the possibility of getting killed by the monster.

Carol placed her thumb and middle finger on one of the four blades and suddenly thought she might hyperventilate. Harold closed his eyes like he was meditating. Carol thought he was pushing down a fresh upswelling of fear, and that inspired her to beg for them to wait just a few more minutes. Before she could open her mouth, though, there was an incredible shrieking roar from outside. Even from a distance and muffled by the earth, the sound made everyone's bones vibrate.

Harold opened his eyes and turned to Carol. "I've shut off the cloaking spell."

"Here she comes," said Snake cheerfully.

Harold said something. For one psychedelically confusing moment Carol thought she'd had a stroke, because all she heard coming out of Harold's mouth was gibberish. Then he fixed a hard glare on the prayer wheel and she realized this was it, and that she was supposed to be spinning and repeating.

She began to spin the wheel. Immediately she felt panicked because it seemed impossible that she could be spinning it in the slow steady way Harold had insisted on, after starting with such a jolt of terror. But when she looked she saw that, actually, somehow, she was doing it precisely the way he'd instructed.

And even though she'd thought she could never remember the nonsense he'd just spouted, when she heard herself talking she simply knew, somehow, that the syllables coming out of her mouth exactly matched those which had just left his: "Moheetam podayyat kruul," she said.

"Faheetam keerass pang," he said, as the wooden door behind and above them exploded inwards and sent a stinging rain of splinters against their backs.

There came that roar again, as hideous as the night before. As the sound waves rippled through the air they twisted its molecules in weird, unnatural ways. Carol wasn't sure if she could really feel the monster's cold breath huffing against her neck, or if that was only her imagination. "Faheetam keerass pang," she said, spinning the prayer wheel like it was no big deal.

She kept her concentration on Harold's face, but in her peripheral vision she took note of Snake, too. The older woman was pointing her gun at the thing behind them. Carol thought it was odd that she was only holding the gun with one hand, and her left hand at that. Maybe she was ambidextrous.

"Kweephat mogum harag deela," said Harold.

You've got to be kidding me with this shit, thought Carol. She repeated the mumbo-jumbo as best she could. It seemed impossible that she could be getting it right, but she must have been close enough; behind her, the monster shrieked again, but less blastingly loud this time, and shriller, and with a note of desperation. Plus Carol figured they must be doing something right, or they would have been smashed already.

Maybe it was wishful thinking, but Carol thought her hopefulness was confirmed by Harold's expression, which seemed much less terrified than a few seconds earlier. Almost triumphantly, he intoned, "Magwassa keemaha hegeilphlat purdoosan!"

Carol began to repeat it. But she never finished.

She broke off in shock as Snake suddenly leapt to her feet and lobbed something over their heads at the monster behind them.

"Keep chanting!" shrieked Harold. "Keep chanting! Keep chanting!"

Carol tried to snap herself out of it and pick up where she'd left off. But then the words fled her mind as Snake began spraying gunfire over their heads, and the conjuration roared anew, louder than ever—so loud this time that Carol lost her hearing for a second.

When it faded back, through the din she heard Harold demanding with a sobbing shriek, "The fuck are you *doing*?! What the fuck are you *doing*?!"

"You said you could theoretically control this old gal if we softened her up first. Well, I tossed some of those submission gourds into her, so man up and make that theory practice."

"Those aren't Gourds of Submission! They're Gourds of Force!"

It was the first time Carol ever heard Snake at a loss. "They're what kind of gourds are they?"

"Idiot! Idiot! Idiot!"

The monster roared again. Even louder now, its force compounded with rage, its strength augmented by the Gourds. It sank in for Carol that the ritual was over, and she sprang forward.

Just in time, too. The monster had forced its way through the narrow opening far enough that it was able to thrust its neck far into the cellar, and when Carol spun to look behind her she saw a demonic version of her mother's face snapping at the air where she'd just been. Apparently there was a limit to how far the neck could stretch, because it stayed more or less where it was, facing them and snapping viciously. But a quick glance up revealed that the roof was bending around the edges of the trapdoor where the thing was forcing itself inside.

Carol shrank from the thing partly because it was trying to kill them and partly because it had her mother's face.

Harold was yanking his hair and crying. Snake pulled an object from one of her endless pockets, plucked something out of it, and threw it at the monster. Carol turned to follow its trajectory, and saw it fly past the head and disappear into the thing's lightning-flushed body. It sank in like it was entering thick water, leaving slow ripples behind.

Harold paused in his fit. "Was that a grenade?"

"Duck and cover!" shouted Snake. Carol was about to ask what she should duck behind, when the explosion came.

Earth collapsed into the cellar. Snake must have ignored her own advice to take cover, because she was there to grab Carol and snatch her away before a few hundred pounds of dirt, stone, and timber collapsed onto the spot where she'd been.

Carol didn't understand why they weren't all dead. The explosion had caused a big part of the roof around where the monster had been to cave in; meanwhile the monster had recoiled. The grenade must have hurt it.

"Move, assholes!" shouted Snake. Carol realized that the slope of the collapsed earth formed a kind of crude ramp, and that the monster had left a space free where they could escape. When Snake shoved her, Carol started running up the slope, wondering what the hell she was going to do once she got out.

Only now did it sink in that Snake had tried to capture the conjuration, even after Carol had told her how she felt. "Fucking *traitor!*" screamed Carol, but instead of berating her any more continued up the ramp, trying to stay alive.

Harold was scrambling up beside her. When his foot slipped, she automatically reached out to steady him, but he waved her off with a frightened squeal.

They were up the ramp. Night had come, and almost the only illumination came from the phosphorescent creature itself. It saw them, though. The neck had been retracted, the face now a relief bulging from its front, forming something like a snout. The glaring howling visage darted at them.

"*Hold!*" cried Harold, flinging his hands in the thing's direction as he had done the night before. Again a barely visible, glimmering force-field popped into being just in time to prevent the creature from dropping all its weight onto them and rending them apart. Instead it bounced off, with that same odd, distant whumping sound.

After that bit of exertion, it looked for a moment like Harold wasn't going to be able to stand back up. As he crouched there, wheezing and trying to regain his breath, Carol once again unthinkingly reached out to take his arm.

He pulled it back. "What's wrong with you?!" His voice was so weak, shrill, and scared that it was almost physically painful to listen to it. "I told you what'll happen if we touch each other again!"

"I don't *know* what's wrong with me! I ought to leave you to fucking die! Anyway, we already touched each other the other night, asshole. I thought that was how this all started."

The monster beat itself against the force field again. Then there was more deafening gunfire, and Snake's voice shouting. "Yo, bitch! Come and get me!"

The monster might have been more interested in Harold and Carol than in Snake. But for the moment its animal mind couldn't figure out a way past the force-field (the shield was floating in mid-air, so it could have just slithered its neck under the edge), and the gunshots aggravated it. It dove back into the cellar to console itself with the more accessible prey inside, before returning to glut itself on the main victims later.

Carol felt a stab of pain at the realization that Snake was about to die. What got her moving again was the sight of Harold, running, slipping away from her.

She took off after him. "Stop! Stop, you motherfucker!"

He spun around, both hands out, dancing backwards away from her. "Don't *touch* me!" he cried. "Our signal is slowly fading— it's getting harder and harder for the conjuration to track us. But it'll come back as strong as ever if you touch me again!"

"I'd rather get eaten by that thing than let you escape, motherfucker."

Behind them the Refuge exploded. Carol and Harold were knocked down. The monster screamed, caught in the firepit. More screams from the monster.

Harold was up and running again. At least this time he paused to look back, waved his hand for her to follow, and cried, "Come on! Jesus, hurry!" She scrambled upright and obeyed.

By the time she reached him he had opened what seemed like a door into the earth itself. It looked like it was made of dirt and it had grass growing out of its top. As she skidded to a stop she tried to peer inside for a closer look, but Harold started shrieking, "What are you doing?! Get in! *Get in before it sees us!*" Carol dove into the dark hole; there was a rough wooden ladder, but between the darkness and her frightened haste she lost her balance and tumbled onto the dirt floor. Above her the square illuminated by the multicolored fires outside disappeared, and Carol understood that Harold had shut this second trapdoor.

There was the noise of him clambering down the ladder. A few rungs from the bottom he stopped, and hissed, "Where are you? I don't want to bump into you!"

She rolled out of the way so that he could finish coming down the ladder. For a while she just lay there listening to him gasp as he regained his breath at the foot of the ladder, and listened to the monster's screams outside. At last Harold muttered "Lux fiat," and a dim glow radiated out mysteriously from a point in the darkness near the middle of the room. As far as illumination went it was pretty pathetic, but it was enough for Harold to find his way to an old-fashioned kerosene lamp hanging from the low wood-beamed ceiling without touching Carol.

The magical glow was already fading by the time Harold got the lamp lit. His hands shook, his flesh was moist with cold sweat, his breath was raggedy; Carol was getting used to the idea that he was a coward, but this seemed like more than a loss of nerve. All this shit was taxing to him. What with the ritual that Snake had interrupted, then creating that force-field, and now with that weak little light he'd summoned as the final straw, Carol wondered if he wasn't about to collapse.

And she wondered how she was going to survive if he did.

He sat heavily on the dirt floor, leaning against a wooden pillar. Carol looked around. It was hard to tell the size of the space in the flickering yellow kerosene light, but she could see that it too was filled with shelves crammed with knick-knacks.

She didn't let Harold spend more than a few seconds getting his breath before she said, "How many of these bunkers and cellars and Refuges do you have sprinkled around?"

After one more gasp, he said, "It's a secret."

"Okay. Whatever. So what now?"

It was a struggle for Harold even to speak. "Tell you tomorrow. Let me sleep."

She was tempted to tell him that he could explain now. But he was clearly at the end of his rope, and she did need him if she was going to live—especially with Snake gone. So if he claimed he needed rest, she had better let him have it.

61

But there was one question that was niggling at her too much to let it go: "How come you're scared of Snake?" she asked. "I mean, you can conjure a force field to keep that big monster away from you. How come you couldn't protect yourself from me and Snake? How come you couldn't stop her from throwing those gourds into the conjuration?" Harold grimaced, like the question annoyed him and he was trying to think of a way out of it, and Carol's temper flared: "Hey, jerk! I already don't trust you, and if you're going to go around keeping secrets it's not going to help!"

"Don't I have the right to some privacy?" complained Harold, then quailed under her glare. "All right, all right. That coven—when they helped me, they did it under certain conditions. And the main one was, that I can no longer use any magic against human females. So you guys are safe from me."

While Carol was processing that, she suddenly heard Snake's voice! Thin, muffled by all the intervening earth, but there nevertheless: "Guys? Hey, guys?" True to form, she sounded like she was having a pretty good time out there. "Hey, guys, where you at?"

"Snake's alive!" said Carol. "We have to let her in!"

He stared at her. "Keep your voice down!" he hissed. "What if she hears you? Of course we can't let her in! She wants to use us to lure that thing to her and capture it!"

Oh, yeah. Carol blushed. Yes, that had been a pretty stupid knee-jerk reaction, she reflected. She'd been so happy to be freed a moment from the same old guilt that had been following her around her whole life: that of having failed to protect the person who was supposed to be looking after her.

And now she blinked back tears at the memory of Snake's betrayal. She supposed Snake hadn't actually come out and said she'd respect Carol's wishes, exactly. Still, this proof of how little Snake cared cut her. Of course, it was stupid for Carol to have thought Snake might "care"; she didn't know what had led her to that misapprehension, and her tearful feeling was in part spurred by embarrassment at her own stupidity.

Harold kept a sharp eye on her until he was sure she wasn't going to, say, open the trapdoor and hail Snake. He curled up on the floor and began snoring within seconds.

Carol tried to listen for Snake, but heard no more from her. Soon she, too, was having trouble staying awake. But then she remembered that she had spent most of the day asleep, and shouldn't be tired. As soon as it occurred to her that there might be something supernatural about her fatigue, she became frightened by it, and struggled to claw her way back up to full consciousness. But it was no good ... it was like her mind had lead weights attached ... and they were dragging her down, down into darkness....

Eight

Except it wasn't dark where she ended up. So many of her dreams took place in forensic brightness.

She was in a bathroom. After a moment's disorientation, she figured that out. The freezing, hard thing she was sitting on was the toilet lid. The bright white surface of squares before her was a wall of ceramic tiles. There was a sink, and above it a mirror. There was something disquieting about the mirror, and after a moment she realized she saw no reflection in it. If there had been a reflection, what would it have looked like? Carol wasn't sure, because she couldn't remember what *she* looked like.

Also there was the tub.

That was the only part of the room that was not bright. It was filled with something viscous and dark and still, something almost black. A reddish black; now Carol understood that it was blood. She noticed a corpse reclining in the tub of blood. Carol couldn't really see the corpse's face—she wasn't certain whether that was because the face had been torn off, or because for some reason her eyes wouldn't focus on it.

"What do you think?" asked a cruel voice, from over Carol's shoulder. She spun around to look up at the speaker—her first reaction was to think, with a thrill of fear, that it was her mother talking. But then when she saw the speaker, it was Harold, smirking down at her. Why had she thought it had been her mother's voice she'd heard?

He was wearing a dark blue, crisp policeman's uniform. The silver badge on his chest gleamed in the fluorescent light, and he stood cockily with his thumbs hooked inside the front of his black leather belt. Weapons and other strange accoutrements hung from it.

"What seems to be the problem, little girl?" he asked.

Carol was wearing that frilly princess dress from her last dream. In contrast to that one, everything here seemed just slightly oversized.

Vaguely she knew that she ought to be mad at Harold. But he was playing the role of a true bona fide policeman, and her conditioning kicked in enough that she deferred to him. Pointing at the faceless corpse in the pool of blood, she said, "I think that's my mother."

"Yes," said Harold, drawing the syllable out, curling his lip into a sneer.

That pissed Carol off enough to rouse her, a little. "You did this," she accused.

"I sure as fuck did."

She ought to stand up and confront him—she was a coward and a traitor if she didn't. But her backside was like a wet sandbag. "Well, why don't you fucking arrest yourself then," she managed. She hated the way her voice shook, but at least she'd managed to say something.

Now he turned that contemptuous sneer upon her. In the moment before he spoke, she realized she had seen the expression before. "Don't be so fucking stupid, Carol. I'm your mother."

"Oh." Carol dropped her eyes, abashed. On the one hand it didn't seem fair that she be expected to recognize her mom when she looked like her own rapist. On the other hand, it must be a pretty shitty daughter who can't even recognize her own mother.

Harold—her mother, that was—had turned her sneer back upon the face-skinned corpse in the tub of blood. She (he?) glared at it, jaw muscles bunching in fury and vengeance. "Now I've got him," she snarled, with Harold's face and Harold's voice but with a spirit Carol recognized, from her girlhood and her dreams. "Shoe's on the other foot now, bitch."

"Momma. Why are you wearing his face? Don't we hate him?"

"This time he's the one who's fucked. And I'm the one who gets to do the fucking."

"But you're going to watch out for me, aren't you, Momma? I'm just afraid I'll get caught in the middle of it and you'll kill me too."

Her mother (Harold) didn't seem to have heard her. She still stared at the faceless head of the woman in the blood. Her own face twitched and quivered. "Bitch," she rasped. "Motherfucker."

Carol tried again to get her mom's attention, though she wasn't sure she was going to want it or know what to do with it, once she had it. "Momma? I don't want to get killed too, Momma."

At last her mother looked down at her. Sure enough, now that Carol had her mom's attention she regretted having worked so hard to get it. It was Harold's face, but she had yet to see that face look as frightening as it did with her mother's spirit animating it.

Her mother's voice came out thick and ruthless: "Then get the fuck out of my way."

Then her mother reached out with Harold's hand, as if to cover Carol's face. Carol screamed and thus woke herself up.

She quickly remembered where she was: another Refuge, in this second cellar. More like a bunker—the ceiling was even lower, the supporting beams thicker, the light dimmer. In the kerosene glow it was impossible to guess the time. Harold, the real Harold, was sitting cross-legged on the other side of the room. His back was to her, but he had twisted around to look—because she'd startled him when she'd screamed, presumably.

Carol rolled onto her side, facing away from Harold. She curled up, choking down her sobs before they could become audible.

Once she was calmer she cleared her throat, stood, and walked over to Harold. He must have heard her approach, but didn't turn to look; he was concentrating on something.

She waited for him to volunteer what he was doing. When he continued to ignore her, she said, "What's up?"

He finally looked up, with a gasp of exertion, and she saw that once again he shone with perspiration. These last couple days had been pretty hard on the guy; she accidentally felt a moment's sympathy, before reminding herself how much she hated him.

Once he had his breath back, he said, "Well, it didn't work out with the Tuvokians and the prayer wheel, so we're moving to Plan B. Under the floor here is an old Indian totem. Its power is why I originally chose this site to build another Refuge. I've set a digging spell to extract it. Hopefully it'll have enough juice to enable us to fight the conjuration—though it would have been easier with the prayer wheel."

Carol was frowning. "An Indian totem? You mean, like, to do with Vishnu or something? Here? Why would an old Hindu thing be buried in the US?"

"Oh my God. Are you kidding me? Fine, a Native American totem."

"Oh, okay...."

"Of all the times to worry about being politically correct...."

"Okay, I said okay! I just misunderstood is all!" She looked at the patch of dirt floor in front of Harold. Because the light was so dim, she hadn't noticed till now that something funny was happening there: it looked like a very slow, very shallow whirlpool was turning in the dirt. "What the heck is that?"

"That's a digging spell. We can't just use shovels to dig it up. If we don't take the time to use magical means, the totem's spirit will decide we're uncouth barbarians, and will abandon us to our petty fleshly problems."

Carol threw her hands up. "Jesus, what is it with all these touchy spirits?!"

Harold hissed and waved his arms. "Shhh! Even saying *that* could offend the spirit!"

"All right, all right." Carol sat down next to Harold as he explained how the totem spirit was not only touchier but also more reticent (lazier, basically), meaning that whereas the Tuvokian spirits were willing to do all the work as long as they were asked in the proper way, Harold and especially Carol were going to have to carry a significantly greater portion of the weight this time.

"What does that even mean?" she asked.

"It means that it's not going to be enough for you to simply have power within you available to be tapped, like we were planning with the Tuvokians. You're going to have to actually guide and direct it, like a real witch."

"Yeah, well, I don't know how to do that."

Harold got flustered, and seemed unwilling to look at her. With a shrug, he said, "Well, I'll just have to teach you."

There was a pause. Carol got the impression he was waiting for her to unload hot wrath on him. That's exactly what she planned to do, too. But she found herself holding her tongue.

As the silence lengthened, Harold snuck a cautious look at Carol. He ventured to speak again: "I know I'm not a guy you want to hear this from. But you remind me so much of your mother."

Again there was a pause, before Carol said, "How am I like my mom?"

"I told you before. The quality of your power. Its aura, the flavor of it."

Another pause. Without looking at him, she said, "Tell me about this retreat or whatever, where you met my mom."

"It was in the Catskills. A big gathering. A bunch of mages and witches were assembled to raise a Blorinang. That's an inter-dimensional immortal spirit. Technically it's a type of demon, but really they're harmless. Anyway, almost none of us had ever met before, but your mom rode up with a friend of hers. God, I'll never forget the moment she stepped out of that car! You might potentially have as much power as her, but hers was developed, trained. And so pure and bright. Like a sun hanging round her neck and shining out of her sternum, except a sun you could stare into. Like she'd swallowed a star and its glow was leaking out from all her pores. So beautiful."

"And then you raped her."

She said it like a challenge, like she wanted to see whether he would dare to keep talking or whether he would shut up and fold. He did keep talking; "Yes, I raped her," he said, and before he spoke she noticed the hint of a pause. It reminded her of a woman she'd met who'd been through Alcoholics Anonymous, of the way she had almost imperceptibly steeled herself before launching into discussions of her dark days. Again, it infuriated her to see Harold giving himself the leeway to own up to his sins in such an oh-so-adult fashion, but it also threw her off-balance and rendered useless all the scripts she'd spent years preparing.

He continued: "I told you, there was a spell I was determined to cast, an evil spell, one that would have let me control minds and raise an army of the damned. Raping your mother was the first step. As the process went on, I discovered that the cost of the succeeding steps was even steeper, and steeper and steeper, and I couldn't pay. That's why throughout history there aren't periodically dark empires policed by armies of the damned—that's a lure thrown out to attract suckers like me, to trick us into giving up our souls." He must have seen in Carol's frown that she was trying to imagine how the rather plain Harold had ever been able to picture himself as a dark emperor, for he blushed. "Deep down I knew I was getting out of my depth. That was the point. I knew how small I was. That was why I wanted to become bigger, greater."

"If you're going to talk then tell me about my mother. I don't care about you."

"Your mother wound up where I started. Small. Reduced. Diminished. But when she began she was very different. Since the conjuration's first appearance, since that first attempt at revenge, I've realized that raping your mother might have been the very worst thing I ever did. Because what is revenge but a lust for power? The power to reset the universe? To erase the past? To regain the strength that I'd destroyed?"

"That's a very convenient line of bullshit," sneered Carol. What the fuck else had the guy done, if raping her mother only *might* be the worst?

"Maybe you're right," admitted Harold. "What matters for the moment is surviving the conjuration."

Part of Carol wanted to stick to this subject, until she'd forced him to say some of the things she'd been longing to make him say. Instead she said, "You told me I was going to have to be more active in the magic stuff this time."

"You'll have to basically take charge. I'm almost tapped. And besides, I never did have the same level of power that you do, if you only knew. That's another way you're like your mother."

Carol didn't reply, but Harold must have seen the angry resistance in her face. He said, "I know I'm not your guru. I told you that before. But right now I'm all you've got."

For a while she only continued to glare hard at him, mouth bunched up. At last she said, "Fine. I'll let you tell me about my mother. About how to be like she was, before."

Nine

How had Snake escaped the night before, from the rampage of the monster? Well, she was a true professional, and every trade has its secrets. Suffice it to say that she had a number of tricks always ready up her sleeve.

The merry chase she and the big glow-in-the-dark bitch had run through this clearing had trampled any sign of Harold's and Carol's passing, so she couldn't track them. But she didn't see any bits and pieces of them spread around anywhere, and the big girl was transparent so she assumed it would have been obvious if they'd been eaten. Not that she had her in view at the moment—Snake had retreated into the woods and clambered up a tree, letting the big girl roar it out below. Snake had finally caught some sleep while up in that tree, since sleep had to happen sometime, even for her.

Altogether, she got about four hours of shut-eye, mixed in with periods of thinking and planning. At one point she was snapped awake by a sound like a skyscraper collapsing. It didn't seem to have come from the immediate vicinity of her tree, though, so she went back to sleep.

At dawn she climbed down and began tracking the big girl. In some ways it was easy; in some ways, hard.

Finding where the creature had charged into the woods was pretty easy—she'd knocked down a bunch of saplings and banged some really big-ass trees into wonky angles, scraping the bark off their sides as she went. At first Snake thought she was going to be able to just follow the highway the thing had tunneled through the woods till she reached the creature (at which point she'd have to speedily figure out what to do next).

But after the first bend in that tunnel, Snake was taken aback to find that it all ended in a curtain of trees, as if the big girl had all of a sudden become immaterial. Which, she realized, was exactly what had happened.

After that she spent hours wandering the woods, looking for spots where the trail reappeared, trying to gauge how long the sign had been there, trying to put it all together into a pattern of the creature's wandering. Sometimes she would hear the creature roar in the distance and she would rush toward the sound, always keeping a careful eye out for Harold's booby traps. But she never managed to catch sight of her.

She spotted more of Harold's tripwires, as well as patches where she could see that the ground was just camouflage covering a pit—when she moved aside the camouflaging grasses and branches and peered into one of these pits, she saw that its bottom bristled with nasty punji sticks. But the big girl never fell through any of these camouflaging mats, even when her trail led right over them. And for the most part she didn't trip the wires, either, although sometimes she did—the curved impaling sticks had been released without seeming to affect anything, as when Snake had provided her demonstration to Carol. Snake couldn't figure out by what system the big bitch sometimes was and sometimes wasn't material, and the question fascinated her.

There was a chance that she would come upon the remains of the kid, pinned against one of these trees. But Snake doubted it. Presumably, Harold had taken her off to some little hideout, since he seemed to think he needed her mojo to neutralize the big girl. Snake had a feeling the kid could take care of herself, and she felt confident she would be able to find the new hideaway. She just wanted to get a better idea of the big girl's behavior first.

Once the sun rose to the middle of the sky Snake took a break, feeling the sunshine pressing down on her, listening to the ubiquitous cicadas' raucous, monotonous party. About time to head back to the clearing, she figured. To the ruins of the cabin, to the abandoned Refuge, and to whatever new bunny hole the guys were hiding in. Time to accept that she was going to need Harold's help to figure out the big girl.

The kid would cooperate, with a bit of persuasion. And she wasn't worried about Harold slipping away—the kid would do whatever it took to stop him from escaping, including grabbing him by the scruff and setting off a red alert in the big girl's skull.

Snake's best bet for getting a leash on this thing was to forcibly recruit Harold into helping. It was rough to pull herself away from the woods, was all. Tracking it was such fun. Time to get serious, though. She started back toward the clearing.

Along the way, something caught her eye.

She came to a halt, peering through the screen of trees and underbrush. In the first millisecond she thought something had been caught in one of Harold's traps, but she knew her business too well to persist in that error for long.

She stepped through the tangles of dead branches, ivy, and old leaves.

Tossed into the bushes was the ripped-off head of an eight-point buck. Its black eyes and snout were wide open with shock. Meat and fur dangled from its dirty wound; on the buck's left side the tear started high up on the neck, almost at the jaw, but then descended at a sharp angle so that much of the animal's right shoulder was still attached.

Snake laughed and shook her head in admiration. A few yards away she saw what was left of the buck's body. "God damn, girl," she said, and pulled an apple from one of her pockets and chomped into it. Gripping an antler in one fist, Snake absently dragged the head along behind her while she walked to the rest of the corpse, as if the head were a souvenir she were going to hang onto.

As she neared the rest of the tattered body, she slowed down. And as she took the last few steps, she saw around the corner of the trees a sight that made even her stop and stare.

Snake found herself staring down a massive trench that had been shoved through the forest. It stretched on for a half-mile; well over a hundred trees had been toppled, and most of them were lying flat, facing the same direction, though on the peripheries of the trench some had fallen into the woods, where most were propped up by their still-standing fellows. At the end of the half-mile, the big girl must have become immaterial again; there was no sign left of the force that had barreled through here, chewing up this stretch of the forest.

Well, Snake had definitely found where last night's terrific noise had come from.

Now she knew for sure that the creature could change size. When it had come through here, it had been a shitload bigger than the last time she'd seen it.

Snake grinned and took another bite out of her apple. "You are so fucking boss," she said, under her breath.

Back at the clearing she began studying the ground more closely than before. As she'd expected, there was no trace left of Harold's and Carol's passage—the whole area around the Refuge had been torn to shit, and the creature had gone on a screaming rampage over most of the rest of the clearing.

Still, Snake was sure there was another hideaway or two around here. And not far away. It would have been too big a pain in the ass to dig one in the woods, where he would have had to deal with all the fucking roots and shit. Unless he'd done it by magic, she supposed.

Harold and the kid were scared of the big girl. Well, that was natural. But Snake knew that animals didn't respond to fear. They responded to discipline, and respect. It didn't matter how much bigger and stronger the thing was; Snake felt sure that the animal would bow to the stronger will, once she'd been made to understand that the will was stronger. Any human ought to be able to outwit a beast, even if the average human was too scared and under-confident to realize it.

It would help if the big girl understood that her new master's plans were in line with the animal's own inclinations. Snake felt sure she could express that to her. Like transmitting your mood to a faithful dog.

She recalled two years ago, when some targets had turned the tables on her and she'd spent two weeks being hunted through the Gobi Desert. Goddam, if only she could have had that big girl with her then! She imagined those smug bastards' faces if she had been able to conjure that fucking beast out of thin air.

As she moseyed around she heard the air split as somewhere off to the west that big bitch let out another holler. Snake froze, her heart knocking inside her, and she had an almost uncontrollable urge to light out after the thing. Like she'd said, Carol could take care of herself against the creep. And sooner or later someone out there was going to hear the old girl and come investigate. It was going to be enough trouble wrangling her under control as it was, without outsiders poking around.

But with an effort she kept herself under control. Their little friend had bought up all the land in a big circle for fifteen miles in any direction, with his cabin in the center—being a warlock must pay pretty good, she reckoned. From the sound of her roar the big girl was nowhere near that perimeter yet. And anyhow, she was the one creature Snake had ever matched wits with that Snake couldn't track, what with her constant fading in and out of existence.... No, if Snake was going to get a handle on her, she was going to need Harold.

So she kept looking.

It didn't take her long to find something: a trapdoor. She was a little embarrassed not to have spotted the anomaly during last night's running to and fro; on the other hand, the creature had been trying to kill her. And this trapdoor was disguised well enough to fool most observers: a patch of grassy sod had been laid atop it, the grass the same color and length as the surrounding vegetation.

Snake spent a second deciding how to proceed. There was no guarantee her bunnies had run away down this particular hole; there could be other safe-houses sprinkled around, although at a certain point it would start to get ridiculous.

Regardless, it would be nice to take a gander inside of this one. Snake supposed she could just blow the door off—she still had explosives packed away in her pockets and utility belt, and could manage a controlled blast that probably wouldn't kill anyone within.

She had other stuff in those pockets too, though. And it might be useful to see what those two were up to, if they were in there. Would also be nice to know what they were saying.

Like she'd told Carol, she had already tested for electronic surveillance (another trick of her trade) and hadn't found any. As for whether Harold was keeping tabs on everything she did via some sort of crystal ball, she could only hope not. It had seemed like he'd been able to sense her when she'd first tried to sneak up on the cabin, and he'd run out with his shotgun; but now he had his hands full and was nearly tapped out, so maybe he didn't have enough bandwidth to keep an eye out for her.

Getting down on her hands and knees, she felt around the edges of the camouflaging sod, trying not to make any noise. She took a thin wire from her pocket, that split in two at its tip like a wishbone. Upon each of its two ends was a small plastic bead, one glassy, both black.

Snake worked the two tiny balls in through the tight crack between the trapdoor and the surrounding earth. She did it slowly, to avoid attracting the attention of anyone below. She could tell when the end of the wire was freely out in the open beyond the trapdoor, because there was less resistance. Her end of the wire was connected to a transmitting device—its plastic casing was black and about the size of a wallet. If Harold or Carol investigated the wire, or simply noticed it as they were coming aboveground through the trapdoor, there wasn't much Snake could do to keep them from finding the transmitter attached to it. But she went ahead and buried it (in shallow ground, so as not to interfere with the signal), in order to prevent some animal from running off with it.

Then she headed back to the cabin. Parts of it were still standing, enough to provide some cover. Anyway, it would make as good a base as any; Snake wasn't particular.

Back in its ruins, Snake took out her smartphone and set it up to receive the signal from the transmitter, a hundred yards away. As she worked, she was aware of the glittering wall of the otherwise invisible force-field. Maybe it was just the effect of seeing it in daylight, but the glittering seemed fainter now; sure enough, when she walked over and cautiously put her palm up to it and pressed, she felt it give. Remembering how the big girl had bounced off it the other night, she was willing to bet it hadn't had this same give then. It seemed to her that the creature would have been able to get through *this* force-field.

Snake took this as a good sign. To her, the takeaway was that this magic stuff was not infallible or invincible. Therefore the creature, being magic, could be controlled. And therefore Harold the Warlock was not invincible either, which meant she'd be able to *make* him show her how to control it.

Not that she hadn't already had plenty of confidence that she could force Harold to do whatever was needed, once she got her hands on him.

She sat down again with her smartphone and lent her attention to the feed being piped in by the miniature camera and microphone she'd snuck into the bunker. For it was indeed a bunker—she could see that on her screen. And through her earbud she could hear Carol and Harold.

She couldn't yet see them, though. She used the controls of the customized app she'd commissioned to slowly move, with infinitesimal micro-motors, the tiny camera inside the glassy bead. She held her breath, worried that the pair might hear the faint whisper of the camera's moving parts. But their conversation gave no hint that they noticed anything at all. Nor did the visual, once Snake had them within the scope of the fish-eye lens.

She watched the show. Took another apple out of her bag and bit it. She'd thought about taking some of that deer meat, but preparing it would have taken too much time. As far as Snake was concerned she was going to be out of here within twenty-four hours. Or dead, maybe.

Off in the distance the creature roared again. In its cry Snake could hear a yearning which matched her own. Once more she had to fight the urge to drop everything and go look for the thing. There was so much they could do together—they could really take the world by storm. Fuck up a lot of assholes.

She returned her attention to the screen of her phone. These two were her best hope of getting the girl on a leash, so she had best pay attention to what they were up to.

Once she did, she laughed out loud. Bits of apple sprayed from her mouth, and she used her finger to push back in the wet crumbs that had stuck to her lips. "What the hell are you bunnies doing?" she mused to the screen.

It looked like they were down there doing a yoga meditation.

Ten

If Snake's first reaction had been to think they looked silly, Carol would have been inclined to agree.

She and Harold were sitting cross-legged facing each other, their spines straight, resting on their sacra. Like many young women, Carol had done enough yoga to know what her sacrum was, but when Harold had instructed her to sit on it she'd been mildly surprised that a guy like him knew the word. He explained that it had long been current in mystical vocabularies.

"Look inside yourself," he was saying, in a low, soothing voice. "Close your eyes, and look within yourself. See the bright light shining, behind your solar plexus."

Her first reflex was to dismiss it all as mumbo-jumbo, but the deepening pit in the dirt beside them would have lent Harold credibility, even if it hadn't been for all the other stuff she'd seen these past two days. When she'd awoken the dirt floor had been basically flat, with some force like an invisible clock's second hand clearing the earth from a small circle. Now, a couple hours later, that clock hand had grown, had quietly drilled down about four feet. They had to get up if they wanted to see the bottom of the hole over the rampart of dirt that had been dislodged to make way for it.

Carol couldn't have set an automated digging spell like that. Harold obviously knew stuff she didn't.

So she was willing to sit in a yoga meditation pose, and close her eyes and listen to Harold intone the sort of New Age spiel she'd heard at dozens of yoga studio meditations. But, because it did feel so much like one of the yuppie yoga classes she was familiar with, she had a hard time taking it seriously.

Barely trying to keep the frustrated impatience from her voice, she said, "I don't really see a light."

"It's there," he said. "A yellow light. Yellow like the sun! And a beautiful blue light, up where your sinuses are. Not a cold blue—a beautiful blue!"

Carol had never heard any yoga teacher, even the most enthusiastic, speak with the same joyous abandon as Harold. Frankly, it was a bit off-putting, and would have been even if she hadn't had reasons to want Harold not to ever feel joy.

He said, "Now, concentrate. Visualize. And, keeping your body absolutely still, will the yellow light to move up along your spinal column till it meets the blue light."

"Yeah, well, like I said, I don't see any lights." She opened her eyes. "I don't think this is working. Can we try another tack?"

Harold blinked his eyes open, thrown off-balance. And he had the gall to be annoyed with her; he really was a bitchy little prick, Carol thought. "Uh. Well. No," he said. "This is it. This is the tack. There is a yellow light inside you, and a blue light. You need to concentrate until you see them."

"And then I, what, I juggle them? That's all there is to it, these two balls of light?"

"No, that's not *all* there is to it, that's only the bare beginning. Which I suggest you at least try to master before we run out of food and water!"

Carol hopped up and stalked across the small room in a huff. There wasn't a lot of space, but if she didn't move around she was going to slug the guy.

Harold watched her, uneasily. After letting her pace half a minute, he said, "What is it that scares you, Carol?"

She came to a halt and stared at him. "Getting killed by that monster, for starters."

Harold shook his head. "No. I don't think that's quite true. There's more to it."

Carol just continued to stare at him. Her face shut down some, became even less expressive; but in its way that was as good as a reply.

"I think you're afraid of failing," he went on.

"You're not going to try to play me with some Freudian shit, are you?"

"I don't pretend to be a therapist any more than I do a guru. But you don't need a degree to see it. You're afraid of failing by not killing me, the way your mother would have wanted. Deep down, you still have the erroneous idea that that conjuration is somehow your mother, and you're afraid that the fact that it's trying to kill you means you've failed her. And you're afraid that you're going to squander this great gift she's left you, this powerful magic you've inherited, so to spare yourself the risk you pretend to simply not believe in it. That's three failures you're scared of."

Carol marched up to him. To an onlooker it would have looked like she was about to kick him in the face or chest, but he held himself steady and immobile. Probably took a real effort of nerves. Glaring down at him, Carol shouted, "Quit empathizing with me, shithead! I did not not come all the way out here so that *you* could understand *me*! I came to explain shit to *you*!"

Harold didn't flinch, but Carol could glimpse the fear behind his eyes. That gave her some satisfaction, at least. Carefully, in a low voice, he said, "All I want is to survive. That's all. Or if I do have to die, I want it not to be by that thing out there. In order to live through this I need you. Because you *do* have the power. You *do*."

Carol stared sullenly at him. She wanted to tell him to fuck off, but she also wanted the knowledge he held.

She looked down into the pit. The dirt was still moving itself out of the way under its own power, but it had almost completely revealed the totem: a piece of dark wood, polished and whole despite having spent who knew how many decades or centuries underground. It was decorated with abstract carving that she couldn't make out in the gloom. "So we can't just walk down there and pick it up?" she asked, hopelessly.

"*No*. Please, don't even say that. It would be an affront to the proud spirits if we dared to touch their fetish with our mere hands. You must use the power of your mind."

She didn't reply at first. She wanted to tell Harold he was full of it; but she knew that wasn't true. Part of her simply didn't want to do anything he said. But she knew good and well that, yes, another part of her was plain chickenshit.

Reluctantly she returned to her seat before Harold. "All right," she muttered. "So now what do I do?"

"The first thing you have to do is change your attitude. I know you hate me, and I'm not going to try to argue you out of it. But hate will obscure your power, in this context."

Carol was about to reflexively tell him to go fuck himself, and tell him that he had raped her mother and ruined her life and so she'd hate him as much as and whenever she wanted. But then she stopped herself, because it struck her, with renewed force, that she really did want to live. Of course that had been true all along. It had been true as a given, though; now it was an active hope, infused with all the force of her desire. It wasn't merely that she wanted, in an animal way, to continue existing; she wanted to survive to a point beyond this bunker, to whatever there was on the other side of this vendetta.

And she wanted to know the stuff her mom had known. And to be able to do the things her mom had done. And, fucked up though it might be, Harold was currently the only avenue to that.

"So we can't touch it," she said.

Harold blinked. It took him a moment to switch gears along with her. "Right," he said. "We can't touch the totem with our hands; we have to set it between us here, using only the power of our minds. Your mind, basically. Once it's here, you'll will the conjuration to diminish into nothing. You'll send that desire through the totem, so as to pick up its strength as you go."

"How?"

"How do you raise your hand, simply by thinking about it? Same principle."

Carol chewed on that, then said, "Anything else I need to know? Anything else that might offend the spirits, or whatever?"

"Um. Well, they're probably miffed that we appealed to the Tuvokians first. So any reference to them during the course of our efforts would prompt them to take their ball and go home. But all that means is you shouldn't speak Tuvokian or anything. Not very likely."

"Yeah, no kidding. I can't even remember that gobbledy-gook."

"Okay. Well, let's begin. Sooner or later the conjuration will starve us out. Or your friend Snake will find us."

They got back into position. Straight spine rising from the sacrum, backs of palms resting on knees, and Harold talking about the blue and yellow lights.

Carol grew frustrated, and tried to keep herself from becoming angry; she knew the anger was only an excuse to protect herself from making the effort, a particularly tempting excuse since Harold so richly deserved the anger anyway. "I can't see these lights you keep talking about," she complained.

"You won't, until you decide to. You have to choose to visualize them."

"Well, okay, but then how do I know I'm not just making it up?"

"But you are, in a sense. Fantasy is the first step into reality."

Carol didn't know what that was supposed to mean, but she decided to pretend for the moment that she did.

She closed her eyes. She still strongly suspected that she wouldn't actually see any lights glowing within herself. On the other hand, it was true that she could pretty easily just make them up, so she tried that.

She imagined that she could see the balls of light that Harold kept insisting were there. He told her to move the yellow one up along the front of her spine until it merged with the one inside of her head. She had no idea how to do that, but she just imagined it was happening anyway. As she pictured the two lights smushing together and forming one green glowball, she started to feel funny.

It was like she was going into some sort of trance or something. She tried to shake it off and pay better attention to what Harold was saying, but it was as if the air and time itself had turned gummy.

Sound traveled oddly. Harold was telling her something: to lift the totem, she realized. She wanted to speak, to apologize to him for being so out of it and spacey, but she couldn't because all her concentration was taken up ... by what?

She couldn't say. Almost automatically, she pictured the totem rising up out of its pit, pictured it floating over between herself and Harold, the same way she'd visualized the stuff he'd said to her about the lights. This time, though, she saw it all happening even more vividly. Just when she was thinking to herself how amazing it was that all this was taking place only in her head, she realized that it wasn't—that was the real totem, it really was floating between them, and now it really was hovering there, waiting for her to bring it gently down for a landing.

She stared at the floating object; she thought there might be a happy smile on her face but couldn't be sure she was correctly processing the sensory data being beamed from her mouth muscles back to her brain.

Harold's voice, strangely echoing, wound its way through intervening atoms to enter at her ear: "Don't come out of it all the way," he gently said. "Hold the totem there, suspended. The spirits are dancing all around it, even now. Don't try to see them—they'll be offended. But ask of them our boon. Picture in your mind the conjuration. Send that picture to them. And humbly request of them their aid in saving us from its wrath."

Carol hesitated. What Harold had said was what she wanted, too. But what if that so-called conjuration really *was* her own mother, only in a different form?

"You don't have to spell anything out for them." Now Harold's voice held a hint of nervousness. Maybe he had guessed at her doubts; maybe he was afraid she was going to try to sic the spirits on him, instead. "Just send them your request for aid. While holding in your mind an image of the conjuration. They'll do the rest."

Still Carol paused. Within this trance everything seemed lucid, except for right and wrong.... But she supposed she would ask the spirits to save them, instead of asking them to finally fulfill her mother's vengeance. She wasn't certain that was what the mother she'd always known would have wanted; but she was willing to believe that maybe the mother she *hadn't* known would have wanted it, the mother who'd been cut away and destroyed by Harold's violent act. That mother, she'd decided, she was curious to know something about.

She was about to try doing what Harold had said when there was a strange loud pop that didn't fit the mood. The universe was so muffled that it was hard to be sure, but Carol thought maybe it had been an explosion. All of a sudden there was a dirty, salty smell.

She heard Harold cry out, "Don't get distracted!" And sure enough, Carol realized that she had allowed her attention to be snatched away from the totem, and toward the mystery of that noise. She lurched back for the totem, concentrated on keeping it aloft. Until now she'd been doing whatever she was doing by instinct. At first she feared that bringing to bear the pressure of her intentionality would knock things off-kilter. But she found that she could in fact keep control. And she was pleased. For the first time she felt that there had been more of a purpose to this mission than killing Harold. Evening the scales was still a good, but she felt that she'd also learned something, been expanded somehow. She was ready to request from the spirits that they diminish the conjuration into nonexistence.

Then she heard Snake's voice.

"Um. Moheetam podayyat kruul?" she said.

And then Harold was crying, "No!" And she felt a strange wave of static washing back over her from the totem, and then saw it falling. The instant before it hit the ground, Carol snapped out of her trance.

She blinked, trying to readjust back to mundane sensory input. In front of her, she took in Harold's stricken, grieving face, staring at the fallen totem. Then she turned. Smoke was clearing from under the trapdoor, or from where the trapdoor had been. Now there was only a raggedy hole up there, sunlight pouring through it. Snake's head was there too, poking upside-down through the gap, looking in on them, and pointing a gun their way as well.

"Sorry about the explosion," she said, as Carol recalled what Harold had said about being careful not to speak the other spirits' language. "But I guess I pronounced the Tuvokian right?"

Eleven

Carol struggled, but then Snake punched her and that was that. All she could do was lay on her back and feel the room spin while she listened to Snake subdue Harold. That didn't take long, either. By the time Carol was back in control of her body she was tied to a post. Across the room, ten feet away, Snake was tying a weeping Harold to another post.

"Ah, shut up, Harold," the bounty hunter said, as she bound his wrists behind the beam of wood. His torso was already tied to it, and she'd tied his ankles up as well. She grabbed his ankles and pulled his legs back so that she could truss him, tying a rope between ankles and wrists.

"Sorry to crash y'all's party," continued Snake. "But I got the impression you kids were about to banish my girl out there back into whatever dimension she came from. And I have different ideas."

Carol was wide awake again now, glaring at Snake. "I thought you were working for me," she said.

Snake stopped tying and looked up at Carol. One would have thought she really was offended. "I am," she said. "But you only hired me to go after the guy. And after I've gotten what I need out of him, I leave his final dispensation up to you, like we agreed. As for any goodies we shake from the tree along the way, that's finder's-keepers, hon."

She had finished with Harold and was firming up Carol's ropes. Once they were both immobilized, she returned to Harold and squatted beside him, smiling.

He didn't like the smile. Even more sweat than usual gleamed all over his face and through his thinning hair.

"Now," she said. "Harold. You had mentioned that the creature could be controlled."

Already he was shaking his head. "I said theoretically," he explained, in desperation.

"So come up with a theory."

He started shaking his head again, but before he could say anything she punched him in the jaw. His head snapped so violently that Carol tensed up, certain for a moment that Snake had broken his neck. The older woman knew what she was doing, though, and Harold only blinked woozily. A second ago he'd seemed ready to start weeping, but for now shock put the waterworks on hold.

"Think positive," suggested Snake. "I know it's a difficult problem, but visualize yourself succeeding. You're a smart guy, right? You'll figure out something."

"You shouldn't do it, Snake," Carol said, without much hope. Snake turned with polite interest to listen to what she had to say. "Look how much havoc that thing has already wrought. Imagine if we were in a town, instead of here in the woods?"

Snake nodded, as if that were a very good point. But she said, "Any bronco can be broken. I just need ol' Harold here to put me in the saddle."

She returned to Harold. "Now, you've got all sorts of little hideaways and ratholes around here. And all of them are full of your little doodads and gizmos and pinwheels and coconuts. And since you've spent the last fifteen years up here shitting your pants in terror that our girl outside was gonna come after you, I have a hard time believing that you haven't grabbed every chance you got to collect something that could keep her in check. So how about we skip the long middle part and you just tell me about that."

Harold was mournfully shaking his head. He worked up his courage and said, "No. I can't do that. I'm sorry. If the conjuration manages to kill me and Carol, it'll cease to exist, which means in order to keep it around you'll have to keep us alive. So that's a plus. But as long as we are alive, the conjuration will be determined to get us. If you hide us from it, it'll go on ever more frequent, blind rampages. All the worldly weaponry of all the armies on Earth can't stop it, and there's no telling how long it would take for some coven or band of mages somewhere to step up. The conjuration could do untold damage before that happens. It could destroy the whole country."

"Hey, have you been keeping up with the news? Destroy the country, gee, what a tragedy."

"Be glib if you like. The fate of the world could hang in the balance. I've already done enough damage to enough innocent people in my life, and I refuse to be party to any more." And he stared straight ahead with a brave set to his jaw.

Snake laughed. "Fair enough, man. I guess if I can't break you, it would be silly to think I could break our new pet outside." She grabbed his T-shirt in both fists and ripped it off him.

The heroic set of his jaw evaporated. "Wha, what are you doing?" he stammered, eyes wide. Carol was frozen, her throat dry. She stared at the pale, flabby flesh of his middle-aged torso, patchy with gray fur.

Here comes what you paid for, she thought, with horror.

Snake reached into another pocket. How many pockets did she have, anyway? This one was so small Carol hadn't noticed it. She pulled out a box cutter. Without preamble, she slid the blade across Harold's gut, in a diagonal line from above his left hip to below his right nipple. Harold yowled as the blood oozed.

"Here's the deal, Harold," said Snake. "All your big talk about the fate of the world and how you won't give in and blah blah blah. But see, I buy your junk about how you feel guilty over raping Carol's mom, and about how you made up your mind to turn over a new leaf. And yet with all that coming-of-age stuff, you never turned yourself in. You never looked in on the lady, to see if you'd permanently fucked her up, or to apologize, or to make restitutions. You never checked to see if possibly you'd knocked her up...."

"Hey!" shouted Carol, thrashing and trying to kick her bound feet. "You shut the fuck up!"

"Relax, sugar—just fishing, just trying to get a rise out of him.... Anyway, Harold, my point is that if you were too chickenshit to do that—too chickenshit just to pick up a phone and say 'I'm sorry!'—then I don't see you being brave enough to let me torture you to death." She reached out and took hold of his left nipple, poofing it out from below and holding the edge of her blade against the top; he started emitting a quick, rhythmic keening noise. "I bet you're not even brave enough to let me cut off a nipple," she said. "I certainly bet we won't get to both."

"Wait. Wait," he wheezed. A trickle of blood began to run from the nipple down his torso. "I'll tell you how. I'll tell you how."

"I know *that*, Harold! I'm just wondering how long it's gonna take?" He was weeping; he tried to say something, but it was impossible to make it out through his snuffles. He winced as Snake increased the pressure on the box cutter and the blood flow thickened. "If you say something but I can't understand you, that counts the same as if you hadn't said anything at all."

"There's a trapdoor," he gasped.

"Well, there seem to be a shitload of those."

"Under the floor. In my cabin. Near where you tied me up. The first time, I mean. Not really a trapdoor, just a fake bottom. Take out the floorboards. There's a Mendolian Rouser hidden there...."

Snake stopped sounding amused. "Skip the technical terms, man," she said.

"Like a, a, a rattle! A rattle with a feather tied to it!"

Snake shook her head in annoyed wonder. " 'A rattle with a feather tied to it.' And this'll let you take control of that thing? Get it to do whatever I tell you to make it do? Will you be able to teach me how to use it?"

Harold tried to speak, but at first could only make a few high-pitched, wet sounds. "I'll try," he managed. "I don't really know for sure. Anyway, that's the best I can do, I swear."

Snake regarded her captive, considering him. At last she said, "Hey, you wouldn't be trying to fuck me over, would you? Send me strolling into one of your booby traps?"

"No," he whined. "I'd be too scared of what you would do to me if you survived."

"Hmm. Flattery will get you everywhere. Plus if I do croak y'all will both die of thirst once I don't come back to untie you, so let's hope that's a deterrent."

Snake made Harold go over all the details of how to retrieve this rattle, and describe it minutely. Then she made him repeat all of it three times, to check for suspicious changes or slips that might indicate he was making it up. As Snake was heading back for the hole where the door had once been, she looked down at Carol and stopped. "You look like someone took a real shit on your parade," she said, not unkindly.

Carol didn't reply, or otherwise acknowledge the observation.

Snake hesitated, then squatted beside Carol. "Hey," she said, gently. "I know this isn't going the way you wanted. And I apologize for that, I do. But this is a big opportunity. For both of us, potentially, because I really do like you. We'd make a good team. You could be, like, the Jiminy Cricket. We could take out a lot of assholes with that ol' girl out there. And if you like, you can have final target approval, to make sure that we only hit assholes who really deserve it. There are enough douchebags on the planet that we can make a very nice living, even if we only stick to killing the worst ones."

Carol scowled. "I can never tell whether you're making fun or you're serious."

"I'm always making fun, and I am always serious."

"Well, either way, you can take your offer and stick it up your, up your fat dumb ass." Furious, she felt tears wanting to squirm their way out from behind her eyes. She blinked them back, and tried to stoke her anger hot enough to evaporate them. "Maybe I'm not totally sure what ought to be done with that thing, but I'm certainly not going to help you exploit it. I hope Harold's right and it really does kill us all, if the only alternative is what you want."

Snake nodded, somberly, like she thought that was a respectable position. "Yeah," she said. "I know. It was just a thought. Sorry to make things hard on you. I know this all kinda violates the spirit of the client-hiree relationship, even if I don't figure I've actually broken any of the terms of our contract."

"Well, you sure do know about making things hard on people," sneered Carol. "Right now you're in a good mood. But I guess if you get pissed off enough you'll do me like Harold?"

Snake laughed, like Carol had surprised her. She shook her head and said, "Oh, no, hon. I'm not saying shit won't go south between us, but you'll never have to worry about that, exactly. Not that I'm such a soft touch, mind. It's just, I know I couldn't break you. Or if I did, there wouldn't be enough of you left to do anybody any good."

With contempt, she turned to look over her shoulder. "Not like our friend Harold," she said. He didn't look up but did slouch a little deeper, glistening like a pale bloody candle melting in the heat. "Fate of the fuckin' world's in the balance, and he's too much of a wuss to spare one measly nipple. When men don't need nipples, even."

Once Snake was gone, it hit Carol that she was bone-weary. She hadn't even been awake for long this time. But these vision-dreams weren't really like sleep; it was more like being robbed of her sleep, like her own dreams were rising up in rebellion to force her attention where *they* wanted, to steal the time she needed for rest and use it instead to deliver their cryptic messages.

Messages from her mom, she supposed.

She could tell that Harold wanted to speak, but that he was afraid Snake might be eavesdropping. As if she might be crouching beside the hole, her ear tipped down their way. "What is it, Harold?" said Carol, the fatigue soaking her voice.

He licked his lips and said, "Carol, listen, we have to get out of here before she comes back. She's going to make us touch. That'll call the conjuration and we'll both be fucked."

"But you can just wave your rattle at it, I thought," she said, ironically.

"The point is we're fucked either way! Say we do by some miracle get the conjuration under control. It'll be breathing down our necks the rest of our lives, trying to get loose and kill us. Plus we'll be slaves to your bounty hunter friend. The only other two soldiers in her mercenary army."

"What do you want me to do about it? Untie these ropes with the magical mystical powers of my mind?"

He gave her a funny look. "Actually, I was going to suggest something like that."

"Oh, for Christ's sake."

"You have the power, Carol...."

"If you don't cut it out with that Yoda shit! Besides, even if I did have your shitty fucking power, I don't have the totem. I don't have the pinwheel. I don't have any of the shit you said I was supposed to use my power *on*. So why don't you shut the fuck up about it!"

"Hey, Carol ... maybe keep your voice down, or Snake could hear ... or the conjuration...."

"Fine! Then let's both shut the fuck up!"

For a few seconds that's what they did. But even when she closed her eyes, Carol could *feel* Harold fidgeting. He wasn't going to leave her in peace.

Sure enough, he said, carefully, trying to keep cool but not able to smooth over the frayed edges of his voice, "Listen. Those tools and fetishes, they're only ways to channel the power. Even the spirits are just middle-men. The reason only a witch or a mage or someone like that can persuade a spirit to do her bidding is because it's the witch's power that the spirit is feeding on and siphoning off. The spirit just has expertise in using it. But the raw power itself is in *you*. Once you get some training, you're going to be one of the most powerful people I ever met. And even without the training, you have enough raw force inside you to be able to get us out of this mess, all by yourself. You could handle Snake, and the conjuration. You only have to believe in yourself. With what you inherited from your mother...."

"For. The. Last. Time. Can it with the motivational speaking. I don't have shit inside me, and there isn't shit that I can do." Carol again felt like she would cry, again fought it off. "All I want is to get some sleep before I die," she said bitterly, and squeezed shut her eyes so she wouldn't have to see him.

Harold didn't say anything for a moment. Carol dared to hope he might really leave her alone. But then she heard him spit out, in a mean voice, "Poor little victim."

Carol opened her eyes. "Excuse me?" she said softly.

"Poor widdle thing. Just like your mom. I guess the inborn powers aren't all you inherited from her. All the inherent, tucked-away powers on Earth can't help when deep down you're a loser."

Voice chilly, Carol said, "I think you're gonna want to shut the fuck up."

"Yeah, well, you already said that. And then to back it up and show me you meant business you tried to go to sleep. Pardon me if I don't beg for mercy."

"Hey. I don't need you to reverse-psychologize me, dickwad."

"What *do* you need? Someone to wipe your ass for you? Seriously, you spend all this money, take all this time off to come out here—or did you even have to take time off? I guess you don't really strike me as the employed type.... Anyway, you come all the way out here, and then what do you do? Curl up underground with the guy who raped your mom and cry. Truly pathetic."

Her eyes were red and bulging, the tendons stood out on her neck. Her breathing rasped in the back of her throat and sounded like a growl. If she could have seen herself, she wouldn't have recognized the face staring back. Harold quavered, stopped taunting, and shrank back against his beam, keeping a careful eye on her all the while.

The ropes binding her did twitch, twice, three times. Harold held his breath.

But then they didn't twitch again. Carol collapsed in on herself.

In a low, encouraging tone, that was very different from the way he'd been speaking a moment before, Harold said, "Carol. You were almost there."

She didn't say anything. She just remained slumped there.

Harold tried again. "Hey. Carol, listen. I'm sorry. I was just trying to, you know...." He trailed off.

A few seconds later, even though Harold had already stopped talking, Carol said, "Shut up, please." She said it like an afterthought, a reflex. She didn't have the energy available to make it a plea, or a threat.

And Harold obeyed. Not because he was nice; not because he respected her wishes, or pain. In a situation as dire as this he would have spared Carol nothing, not for the sake of her feelings.

So he must have thought she looked genuinely defeated.

Twelve

By the time Snake returned with the rattle, Carol was asleep. The older woman took the time to stop and regard the girl with amusement, and maybe even pride. "Shit, she really has got nerves of steel, hasn't she? Not like you."

"No," Harold sadly agreed. "Not like me."

Snake shook the rattle in his face and demanded whether it was the right doodad. Harold confirmed that it was; Snake was amused by the way he went into a near-panic at her rattling it, pleading that there would be great risks in using it other than at the propitious moment. But at the same time she assumed that Harold knew what he was talking about—after all, she was banking on it—and so she quit shaking the thing and set it down carefully.

"All right!" she announced with a grin, clapping her hands together and rubbing the palms. "Time for the main event."

Harold tugged at his bonds in a pathetic attempt to get loose without letting Snake notice what he was doing. He said, almost whining, "But it's almost nightfall. Don't you want to wait till daylight? So that if things get hairy we can see what's going on?"

"Nah—can't wait, too excited. While I was out there, I could hear the old girl tramping around out in the distance. I gotta tell you, it almost made me horny."

Harold stared at her, his terror momentarily forgotten in his bewildered repugnance. "What is it about you and that thing?"

"Man, I don't even know. I just feel like her and I could get along. Now, what's gonna happen, this thing is gonna show up and you're gonna shake that rattle at it and tell it some chant to get it to mind you?"

"Well, er, yes, basically, but maybe we could take a few minutes...."

But Snake laughed again and shook her head. "You had all this time to think shit over and prep yourself. You're as ready as you're gonna get, so quit stalling. Just keep in mind that if you can't bring that big bitch to heel, she'll kill you." And before Harold even realized what was happening, while he was opening his mouth to frame another objection, Snake had whipped out a knife, sliced through the rope attaching him to the post, and started dragging him, still trussed, over to where Carol was passed out.

"No need to interrupt the lady's beauty sleep," opined Snake.

Harold began to babble, screech, and thrash: "No! No! I can't do it! I can't do it!"

"Shit," grunted Snake, approvingly, "Carol can sleep through anything." As if Harold had been able to offer no more resistance than a baby, she hefted him over and pressed his slobbery spastic face to the bare flesh of Carol's arm.

Immediately there was a roar, way off in the distance. Harold moaned. Even his moans were shrill.

Carol's cheeks twitched; her eyebrows knitted closer together. But she didn't wake up. It was not the roar of the creature, out here in the external world, which had disturbed her.

A ramshackle mansion alone on a dark plain. Inside, empty. How could Carol know that it was on a dark plain, and empty, when all she could see of it was the dark lightless closet she was locked inside of? She just knew, and never thought to ask how.

The closet was tight and dark and full of rain. The ceiling must have been very high and stuffed with clouds, but she couldn't see because all was black. But although there was no lightning, there was thunder: high above, reproachful, mocking, and strong.

Carol shrank in the cold wet as waves of deep scolding rumbles vibrated her bones. When it paused, she whispered, "Yes, Momma, I know. But I tried."

The thunder answered. It was deafening, even from its dark distance.

Carol humbly bowed beneath it. "Yes," she said. "Yes, I know. But you're not going to kill *me*, Momma. Are you?"

The thunder rolled. It continued a long while this time, mocking and erratic, and it was hard to tell if it had answered Carol's question.

"But I love you, Momma," she said, daring to look up with her blind eyes. "I love you."

Now the thunder belched, roared, and rumbled for the longest stretch of all, ironic and cruel and with that old familiar mockery stronger than ever before.

Carol listened. She let the sound waves permeate her flesh all the way down to the marrow. Long before the thunder had finished, she'd dropped her eyes again, had hunched in her shoulders and hung her head. The cold needles of the rain soaked her, made her heavier and heavier, lowered her core temperature till it was like she was packed with snow.

She waited obediently till the thunder was done. Then she waited a little bit more.

Finally, she nodded her head, slightly. "I see," she said, in a small voice. "I don't blame you. It's been hard for you, too."

She raised her head. Her eyes pointed straight ahead, at one of the four walls that penned her in, which were invisible in the blackness but whose pressure she could feel. "But," she said slowly, "if you don't want me...."

Something was surging up within her. Like lava. An explosion, but she didn't even have time to get scared as she raised her face into the rain and pointed it toward the thunder.

"... then LET—ME—GO!" she cried, and exploded out, out of the closet, and as she flew back across the plain she had just barely an instant to see the dilapidated mansion collapse....

Her eyes snapped open. No disorientation this time—she knew exactly where she was. Her two companions didn't notice that

101

she'd awakened. Harold was in hysterics, and Snake was trying to control him.

"I can't do it! I can't do it!" he was shrieking.

Snake was brandishing a knife in his face. To Carol it looked like the kind of thing you'd use to gut a pig. "You had better figure it out quick," she growled. "Do one of your fucking chants or something."

"I *can't*! I don't have the power!"

"You strongly implied that you did."

"That was to stall you! To buy time! To keep my nipple! It was bullshit!"

Another shriek from that monster split the air molecules. It was still in the distance, but closing fast.

Snake grabbed the hair in the back of Harold's head and jerked it back. She held the point of the knife an inch above his left eye. "Well, you better look inside yourself and find the power within, bro. If not, I'll still leave you one eye so you can watch that bitch chew your nuts off."

"NO!!!"

That was Carol, though she didn't recognize the uncannily echoing boom as her own voice. She wasn't even aware of having spoken. Not that she had time to think about it, for all of a sudden there was a loud bang beside her ear, and something like a vibrating tuning fork sticking out of the post next to her cheek. She looked; it was the knife Snake had been holding. It had flown back toward her too fast for the eye to follow, and had come within a couple inches of pinning her brains to the wood.

She looked down at the ropes binding her. They didn't so much break apart as explode, bits of fiber flinging themselves violently in all directions only to slow and then float down as the air caught them.

Snake was staring back over her shoulder at Carol. "You grabbed my knife out of my hand," she said wonderingly.

"She's got it!" yelled Harold. "I told you, she's got the power!"

The monster's roar was louder as its running feet whittled away the miles. As Carol worked her trembling numb body upright, she held the post for support and felt the rhythmic vibrations of the conjuration's approach. Snake looked her up and down appraisingly. She straightened up too, leaving Harold on the floor to be dealt with later. "Yeah," Snake mused. "I guess you do have the power. Pretty nifty trick, yanking that knife away. But I bet you didn't mean to almost stab yourself in the face with it. And you don't look too steady on your feet right now. I don't think you have much control over this power, Carol. And that means I can still take you."

Carol jabbed a finger in Snake's direction, like a scolding schoolteacher. "You are *not* taking that thing to use as a weapon. I'll let us all die first."

Snake darted in and stunned her with a right jab to the chin. As Carol staggered back into a shelf, blinking past starbursts, she heard Snake say, "Dying is fine. But *don't* put your finger in my face."

The bounty hunter lunged for her, but Carol ducked out of the way. Snake laughed. The rumble of the approaching beast grew ever louder and the bunker was starting to really shake.

"I told you," said Snake. "Don't fuck with me, hon." She was grinning. But it was a serious grin. "Besides, that's your own mom out there! Kinda-sorta. You should be proud of her!"

"It's *not* my mom. And if it is, that's all the more reason to put her out of her misery."

Snake jerked her head to indicate where Harold was staring, rapt, scared, and immobile. "What about your dad? Gonna put him out of his misery too?"

"Fuck you!" screamed Carol. "Don't call him th—" She didn't finish because Snake's fist planted itself in her face, crunching her nose and smashing her lips back into her teeth. Fireworks blew up before her eyes; she was spinning through emptiness; suddenly something was battering her; then she realized that it was she who was battering the floor by collapsing onto it. Coughing in the dust, she forced her eyes open and saw Snake striding away from her, back to where Harold cowered. "Stay down," she warned Carol, then grabbed Harold with one hand

and the latest fetish in another. Leaning her face down into his, she said, "You better start shaking this rattle, son."

A scream ripped through like a tornado siren right here in the bunker with them. The walls were shaking so hard that it was a wonder the ceiling hadn't caved in. A small cauldron flew off a shelf and conked Snake in the head.

Dazed, she spun around, looked up to see if a piece of the ceiling had fallen on her, then seemed to realize that whatever had struck her had come flying in from the side. She locked her eyes on Carol. "Hey. Was that you?"

Carol sent a flurry of objects spraying into Snake. She couldn't have said *how* she did it. But she did will it, and then it happened, so she supposed she was responsible.

Most of the knick-knacks were light enough that Snake could bat them away; there were so many of them, though, that she couldn't keep up, and a few got her. And a lot of those blows were to the head.

"Hey!" said Snake, in her usual cheerful tone but with a sudden ragged quality to her voice. Blood from a cut dribbled into her squinting left eye. "Hey, fuck that thing outside, maybe just you and I could go on the road!" Then something that looked like a crude iron statue of some god smacked into her forehead, and she crumpled to the floor and lay there motionless.

Motionless, except for the quaking that had overtaken the whole room and that now seemed less like the tramp of the monster's footsteps and more like an earthquake. Shelves toppled on their own, with no help from Carol's newfound telekinesis. She scurried on all fours to where Harold was still tied up. The monster screamed, almost upon them. "How do we stop it?!" she shouted, to be heard over the unearthly howls, the rumbling, and the falling shelves.

He shook his wet face. "I can't! It's all you!"

"I don't know how to do this shit! You were supposed to teach me!"

"Too late! And I'm no good anyway! Do it the same way you told all that stuff to keep flying into Snake! The same way you ask your mouth to open when you want to say something!"

104

Okay. Carol wasn't sure she bought any of that, but from the strange cool blue glow seeping through the hole where the trapdoor once had been, she knew the point was moot.

Harold shrieked as her mother's face came into the bunker at the end of its neck, glowing like compacted starshine as it leered sadistically. It made a bee-line for her; Carol had thought that at least it would kill Harold first. Maybe it only came for her because she was between the monster and Harold, but Carol thought the cruel intention in its cold shining eyes said different.

There wasn't time to scream before the creature's head had slammed into her stomach and thrust her across the room to drive her against the wood planks of the wall, knocking her breath out ... but not breaking her back. It was like she had some invisible cushioning both in front of and behind her, which protected her from the impact. But Carol couldn't understand where such magical cushioning had come from.

"You can do it!" Harold screamed. "The power's in you!"

And Carol thought that, well, maybe *she'd* made the cushions appear.

On the other hand, Harold's assurance that "she could do it" might be wishful thinking. Especially since the monster had no trouble pulling Carol back and slamming her into the wall again, this time hard enough to *really* drive the breath out of her, plus knock a few boards off the wall.

Still, it should have killed her. And even though the sight of that face striking at her like a cobra made her yelp in terror, the face didn't reach her but glanced off some barrier that was invisible, except when it shimmered upon impact: it was like the force-fields Harold had conjured. She'd spontaneously generated one around herself. That was keeping her spine from being snapped. It was like being wrapped in many layers of bubble wrap.

Before she could congratulate herself, Harold was screaming a warning—this time he screamed not out of fear, but to be audible over the monster's frustrated, outraged howls: "That force-field won't last! Not if she keeps pounding on it! You've got to finish her, now!"

This was the first time Harold had referred to the creature as a "she," Carol noted. Had he been avoiding the pronoun all along, to keep her from thinking of the monster as her mother, to keep her willing to kill it? *Was* it her mother? Now that the face was snapping and groaning only inches away, staring into her own, Carol had to admit that the pronoun felt right. She didn't know if her mother's soul was locked away inside the beast, but it was clear that the hungry face raging at her own was not simply, say, an impression left by her mother in the ectoplasmic wax. *Something* animated the entity; it was not merely programmed to rage and kill; it had its own, individual *desire* to rage and kill.

But Carol didn't pause to worry about the metaphysics. She could feel her force-field weakening under the creature's attack. She couldn't have explained how she was able to feel it, or where the sensation was located, but it was surely true.

If she was getting information through invisible sense organs whose nature and location she couldn't pinpoint, then it was plausible that she might have other invisible organs. Less passive ones.

She imagined gripping the monster by the top of its neck, where the head sprouted, as well as gripping it by its morphing body in order to hold it still. She didn't visualize grabbing the creature with her hands, or anything like that; she just tried to imagine subjecting it to an abstract but real enactment of the concept "grip."

The monster felt that it was being restrained, and from the way it glared at Carol she guessed it knew who was responsible. The creature howled and thrashed, and shook Carol hard enough to challenge her force fields. In her mind's eye there was something like a power bar in a video game, and it told Carol those shields were running low on juice.

She would have to finish this quick. Not that she had any idea how.

Hypnotized a moment by the sight of her own mother's face, Carol reminded herself that giving up and dying was also an option.

Instead, she held up her right hand, beside the creature's face. Her fingers twitched instinctively into a mudra of her own creation. The monster snapped at the hand and tried to bite it off; the field blocked it, and became indirectly visible as energy crashed across it.

Once the monster realized it couldn't get at Carol's hand, it returned its attention to her face—it couldn't get at that either, but the sight of it seemed to drive it into a frenzy. The existence of Carol's eyes, mouth, nose, so like its own, was an affront to it, and it clearly wanted to shred and liquefy them, as a step toward the extinction of even the memory of its *own* face.

Wisps of fog began to appear from a spot near where the monster's left ear would have been, if it had had ears, tendrils of mist that were drawn toward Carol's right hand. At first these tendrils were invisible—Carol simply imagined them—but even though they'd had their genesis in her own imagination, she was learning not to assume that meant they weren't real.

Those wisps began to visibly unmelt out of the air. Carol could see them, winding and spooling out from near the creature's temple, to fade away again once they neared her hand, as if they'd been swallowed into the field of her influence. The gentle slowness of their motion made a surreal contrast with the creature's frenzy. Carol wasn't certain yet herself what she was doing, but she could tell it was something big, something that required access to a power that until recently she'd had no clue she possessed. She felt horror at her own exultation.

At first the creature didn't notice what was going on. Then a confused note entered its ferocious jabbering. It broke its stare into Carol's face as its eyes glazed, unfocused, wandered ... then all of a sudden it deciphered the message of its senses, realized what was happening—comprehended that it was dying.

If possible, its thrashing became even more violent and spastic. Now, though, it was trying to escape from Carol. Its roar turned into a scream—still of outrage, but of a different sort—

like the outrage of a virile young man realizing his mortality for the first time as he drunkenly careens his car head-on into another vehicle.

The creature struggled and fought. Carol held it fast and continued to draw out and evaporate the wisps of cottony fog. That was the essence that Harold kept talking about, she guessed. She felt herself growing stronger, and felt the creature growing weaker. She insisted to herself that her new strength wasn't power she was cannibalizing from her mother's creation *(from her mother)*—it was just the strength of her inner chakras or whatever the fuck Harold had been trying to get her to go look at in her happy place.

But she couldn't shake the suspicion that, actually, the surge of power she felt did originate in the entity she held trapped before her. She was like a savage head-hunter getting strong and high off the flesh of her foe. Mother-killer.

The monster raged and raged, then slumped. Carol now needed much less force to hold it down. Its seething humped body seemed to take up less space in the bunker, its glow seemed to dull. But most of Carol's attention remained on its face. That was caving in on itself, slightly, but noticeably; its eyes got bigger as their hollows got deeper; phantom cheekbones stood out from its tightly drawn phantom skin. Now, instead of roaring with rage or panic, it begged; it fixed its horrified saucer eyes on Carol's and, as its bulk melted, it babbled its pleas at her, in words that were gibberish but which were also, Carol felt, a real language that she ought to have known but couldn't comprehend.

That was the worst part. Carol's sobs spluttered out of her, and the right hand that was drawing out the creature's essence nearly dropped down to her side. The tears drowning her eyes didn't do her the mercy of blurring her mother's face out of recognition, as the creature grew more and more pathetic and shrunken. Its pleas had turned to high-pitched mewling whines. There was no longer any pretending that the creature was merely an exotic animal of the supernatural variety. Clearly there was a human soul in there. And Carol knew of only one human's it could be.

"I'm sorry, Momma," she sobbed. "I'm really sorry." But she didn't lower her hand or cease to draw out the creature's essence.

The creature started to shudder. Some crisis point was approaching. Its eyes melted away, leaving not skull-holes but a formless curved plane above the fading nose. It opened its thin-lipped mouth and issued an ugly terrified bleat, and then there was a popping sensation and a bright light and Carol rocked back against the wall again.

She blinked. The monster was nowhere to be seen. For an instant all seemed calm. She looked out at the wrecked bunker and its dimly-lit tableau: Harold still tied up and staring at her, Snake still lying motionless.

"You did it," said Harold. Despite all his encouragement, he sounded surprised.

Then the earthquake started.

Carol toppled to the floor. She broke her fall with her arms, but the jolt to her face was enough to remind her that Snake had popped her a good one in the nose. "What now?!" she cried.

She assumed the monster hadn't been eliminated after all, and was about to pop back into existence. But Harold said, "The conjuration's ceased to exist, and thaumaturgic waves are rushing in to fill the void!" Carol had no idea what that meant. She was able to follow his next words, however: "The disturbance could knock down the supports and cave in the whole place! You gotta untie me!"

Okay. She crawled over to Harold, but then stopped before touching his ropes.

"Please!" cried Harold. "It's all right, the conjuration's gone, you can touch me now!"

She realized that she just didn't want to help the bastard. Still, the walls were shaking, the posts that held up the ceiling were starting to creak, and Carol decided to get him out and then worry later over whether it had been a mistake. She rushed over to yank the knife out of the post, and froze as she noticed that Snake was conscious. But the bounty hunter, still dazed, made no attempt to stop Carol from taking the knife. She just shook her bloody head in disgust.

Carol rushed back to Harold and sliced through his bonds. As he scrambled for the ladder out of the bunker she wanted to tell him not to even think about trying to run, but what with the way the room and its ceiling were shaking, there wasn't time. There was a crash like a concrete waterfall—the room filled with an explosion of dust, and a jolt of terror ripped through Carol, because she thought the whole bunker had just caved in and this was it.

But then, as the ringing in her ears died down, she realized that she was still alive, curled on her side and hacking up dust. Somewhere the kerosene lamp still glowed, and cast its yellow glow through the haze of grit.

From up above and behind her (the way out), she heard Harold's voice: "Come on! Before it all collapses!" Apparently, he cared. Surprise, surprise.

She tried to get up and went down again when her knee gave out. Twisted or sprained or something. Still coughing and trying to blink the dirt out of her eyes, she began to crawl over the rubble back to the exit. And stopped when she got to Snake.

This prelude to the complete cave-in had dropped a roof-beam across her chest. Her face was covered in dirt, and there was a new trickle of blood, this one leaking out the corner of her mouth.

She was awake, though, and able to look Carol in the eyes. "Hey," Carol said. "Hey, don't you worry. We're going to get you out of here."

Snake smirked. Again she shook her head, so lightly it was hard to see. "Oh, hon," she whispered. "Go fuck yourself."

Her eyes glazed and all motion ceased. Carol felt in vain at her mouth and nose for any hint of breath, till she finally decided to listen to Harold, who was screaming at her to get the hell out of there. Maybe it was her imagination, but the shaking seemed to have gotten even more violent, so much so that even

110

while crawling she almost fell over onto her side. And she never would have made it up the remnants of that ladder with her hurt knee if Harold hadn't been there to help haul her up, and then to throw her arm over his shoulder and support her as they ran for safety, with the bizarre sliding, crashing sound of the collapsing earth behind them.

Both of them went down after only a few yards. Only once Carol was lying on the ground did she realize it had stopped shaking. But then Harold was tugging on her arm again.

"Come on," he gasped. "All sorts of explosives in there. We gotta get away."

Part of Carol would just as soon have lain there and given up the ghost. When she did force herself back upright, again holding onto Harold for support, it wasn't because she thought life was particularly sweet. It was because she had just murdered what might possibly have been her mother, all for the sake of staying alive, so it would be pretty shitty to give up and die now.

There was yet another boom behind them, as loud as when the earth had caved in but a different quality of sound, less brooding, more violent. Both of them were flung onto their faces and pelted with small rocks and chunks of earth. Carol waited to see if she'd be killed.

Once it seemed she hadn't been, she slowly rolled onto her back and raised herself up on her elbows to look back in the direction they'd come from. The earth was belching fire, blue and green flames, orange and red—it spurted and farted its way up from the earth that tried to smother it, in spumes and geysers of strange gases.

Carol squinted at the pretty colors. "Is any of that going to kill us?"

"We'll find out," Harold said, not bothering to lift his head and look. He sounded even more exhausted than she was.

She turned to study him as he began to snore. It was weird, she reflected, that either one of them should have cared whether the other one lived. Each had very good reasons for preferring the other dead. She supposed that in situations like this, when

111

humans found themselves pitted against a non-human threat, some sort of genetic tribalism kicked in. It made sense for there to be a strong instinct to band together in such circumstances, so as to preserve the species. Bonds might form between the unlikeliest people.

Carol narrowed her eyes and thinned her mouth. Well, the menace was gone now. And when he woke up he was going to find out that shit was not settled between them, not yet....

After they woke up, though … for gravity was pulling her heavy head back to the ground, and sleep was pulling her whole body down into its great dark swamp....

Only sleep, though. The pull might be inexorable, but she could tell it was biological, as well. It was only her rest-starved body, crying out for sleep. Not another strange invasive cipher from the beyond.

As her eyes closed, a smile flickered across her face in the eerie firelight.

Thirteen

When she awoke it was still night. She had no idea whether she'd been out for minutes or hours. The multicolored flames were lower, but they still burned bright enough to illuminate the clearing, and when she turned to look she saw Harold hobbling off. Maybe that was what had woken her up; maybe she'd heard him, or just sensed his flight with one of her strange new senses.

"Hey!" she shouted, rising on an elbow. It came out as a croak.

Harold froze. She saw him cringe, hunch his head into his shoulders—he didn't want to turn around. But he did, slowly, as Carol struggled to her feet.

They faced each other across the gloom of the clearing, lit by the blue and green flames. Finally, Harold said, "You'll want to take it easy on that knee, or you'll do permanent damage." He said it as if her knee injury were the worst thing that had happened, these past couple days. "The shack is still standing, the one where Snake got the prayer wheel. There should be bandages inside, and you can make yourself a brace."

"Where the fuck do you think you're going?"

"Listen. Snake showed you some of those tripwires. Wait till daylight to walk out of here, and *really* watch your step. Carry a stick with you, a very long stick, so you can poke the earth ahead before you step on it. You don't want to fall into a pit."

"Lucky for me that you're gonna guide me out."

"I told you, I don't even know where they all are. I had been planning to hide here on the edge of the woods till you went away, then tiptoe my way out the same way I recommend you do. Let me remind you that you're the trespasser, and that if you do get yourself killed I don't plan to stand around feeling guilty about it."

113

She limped a few more paces toward him, lurching comically. "You're not going anyplace, asshole. You're going to confess. First to me, and then to anyone I can stick you in front of. Remember your oath?"

He laughed. It was not a happy sound. "'My oath.' It gets hard for me to keep up with them all, Carol. A lot of people have believed me about a lot of things, including your mother. I expected you at least to know better."

She lurched toward him again. "You're keeping this promise."

Harold was still standing his ground. He seemed unconcerned that she might suddenly run at him; he must have thought she looked half-crippled, and considering the pain in her knee he might not be far wrong.

"Snake was right," he said. His tone was strange, she couldn't tell if it edged closer to laughter or tears. "I am a coward. You've seen that yourself. And I'm too scared to do what you want, and tell people the things that I did. It doesn't matter about the statute of limitations. I guess I *would* be more scared of jail than of humiliation. But I'm scared of the humiliation too. I'm scared of people seeing me and knowing what I am."

Carol was continuing her laborious, slow, painful process toward Harold. Judging by her limp, there was little chance of her catching him if and when he ran, but he backed up a few paces toward the trees anyway. "You're going to really injure yourself if you don't keep off that knee," he warned, in a nervous, paternal way. "Just let me disappear. I'll never bother you again. If I get my way, I'll never bother *anyone* again. And I can promise you, I won't be happy."

He meant that, but it was also supposed to be a clever joke. It was that, the way he was trying to wow her with his older-guy sophistication and knowing jadedness, which finally tipped Carol over the edge; she charged at him. For a moment he just stared at her, stunned. Her knee screamed at her, shooting blazing swords down her shin and up her thigh. Harold whirled and fled into the trees.

Fury clotted the forefront of her mind, but underneath that, in the calm rational substratum, she was surprised. There was no doubt that Harold was a coward, and she hadn't expected him to actually brave a real run into the booby-trapped night. Maybe facing her scared him even worse than those savage things.

For her part, Carol wasn't scared at all, not of the traps. The one thing she cared about was the closure that had been the object of her quest, and she didn't care what form it came in. Death could be closure, too.

Up ahead, there was a crash—lighter than the ones she'd gotten used to lately. In the middle of it came a strangled yelp, that cut off even before whatever had crashed finished settling.

Now Carol slowed. For a moment she stood still. Oddly, the throbbing in her knee seemed further away than ever, although she'd feel it keenly soon enough.

At last, she began edging forward again. She tried to keep an eye out for tripwires, but in the moonlight it was impossible. Common sense said she should go back to the clearing and wait till daylight to investigate, but she continued even so.

The pit was barely visible as a big black blot upon the ground, until Carol reached its edge. The moon came out from behind a cloud then. And Carol could see down into the hole so clearly, she almost suspected she was unconsciously using magic again.

Harold lay on his back at the bottom of the pit. Curved spikes like tusks sprouted from the ground. He was impaled on two of them: one through his thigh, one through his middle. The blood running from his mouth reminded Carol of Snake, when she'd died. His eyes were wide open. In the silver light his pale gray face almost shone, like the creature's had, and the blood was black.

Her mouth twisted. She said, "I get to have everything."

She stared down at his face till another cloud smothered the moonlight. Then she turned and limped back to the clearing.

STEWART AND JEAN, by J. Boyett

A blind date between Stewart and Jean explodes into a confrontation from the past when Jean realizes that theirs is not a random meeting at all, but that Stewart is the brother of the man who once tried to rape her.

THE LITTLE MERMAID: A HORROR STORY,
by J. Boyett

Brenna has an idyllic life with her heroic, dashing, lifeguard boyfriend Mark. She knows it's only natural that other girls should have crushes on the guy. But there's something different about the young girl he's rescued, who seemed to appear in the sea out of nowhere—a young girl with strange powers, and who will stop at nothing to have Mark for herself.

I'M YOUR MAN, by F. Sykes

It's New York in the 1990's, and every week for years Fred has cruised Port Authority for hustlers, living a double life, dreaming of the one perfect boy that he can really love. When he meets Adam, he wonders if he's found that perfect boy after all … and even though Adam proves to be very imperfect, and very real, Fred's dream is strengthened to the point that he finds it difficult to awake.

BENJAMIN GOLDEN DEVILHORNS, by Doug Shields

A collection of stories set in a bizarre, almost believable universe: the lord of cockroaches breathes the same air as a genius teenage girl with a thing for criminals, a ruthless meat tycoon who hasn't figured out that secret gay affairs are best conducted out of town, and a telepathic bowling ball. Yes, the bowling ball breathes.

RICKY, by J. Boyett

Ricky's hoping to begin a new life upon his re[lease from]
prison; but on his second day out, someone mu[rders his]
sister. Determined to find her killer, but with no id[ea of how]
to go about it, Ricky follows a dangerous path, [following]
clues that may only be in his mind.

BROTHEL, by J. Boyett

What to do for kicks if you live in a sleepy college town,
and all you need to pass your courses is basic literacy?
Well, you could keep up with all the popular TV shows.
Or see how much alcohol you can drink without dying.
Or spice things up with the occasional hump behind
the bushes. And if that's not enough you could start a
business....

THE VICTIM (AND OTHER SHORT PLAYS),
by J. Boyett

In The Victim, April wants Grace to help her prosecute
the guys who raped them years before. The only problem
is, Grace doesn't remember things that way.... Also
included:
A young man picks up a strange woman in a bar, only to
realize she's no stranger after all;
An uptight socialite learns some outrageous truths about
her family;
A sister stumbles upon her brother's bizarre sexual rite;
A first date ends in grotesque revelations;
A love potion proves all too effective;
A lesbian wedding is complicated when it turns out one
bride's brother used to date the other bride.

ease from
rders his
ea how
ed by

Made in the USA
Middletown, DE
06 May 2022